Peace Lilies

A Sweet Ghostly Novella

Margaret Rodeheaver

Will Way Books, Inc.

MACON, GEORGIA

Margaret Rodeheaver/Will Way Books, Inc.
212 Will Way
Byron, GA 31008
www.margaretrodeheaver.com

Publisher's Note: This is a work of fiction. Names, characters, places, and incidents are a product of the author's imagination. Locales and public names are sometimes used for atmospheric purposes. Any resemblance to actual people, living, dead, or in between, or to businesses, companies, events, institutions, or locales is completely coincidental.

Book Layout © 2017 BookDesignTemplates.com

Peace Lilies/Margaret Rodeheaver. -- 1st ed.
Ebook ISBN 979-8-9883976-1-8
Paperback ISBN 979-8-9883976-2-5

Life is not a movie, and you can't wait for the sequel.
Say 'I love you' before you get to 'The End.'
There will *probably* be no second chances.
Then again ...

Contents

Chapter 1

Birdie Ebersole came through her front door and stumbled against something bulky in the entryway. She tripped and sprawled onto the living room carpet narrowly avoiding a header with her husband's old recliner.

"Ow! What the hell was that?"

Martin, Birdie's husband, abandoned the roller suitcases he dragged behind him and bent to help his wife to her feet.

"Turn the light on, will you?" Birdie directed. "The timer must be screwed up again."

She dusted off her purple travel pants and matching jacket, adjusting the sleeves which she wore pushed up almost to her elbows. She was amazed that her body was uninjured, and looked back toward the entryway. "Peace lilies? I hate those damn things. Now I have two of them? Who the hell brought these?"

"I don't know, Birdie," Martin said.

"If they're supposed to be a welcome-home present, they can take them back where they got them."

Birdie gazed around at the rest of the house. "I see that son of yours did his usual stellar job of looking after the place while we were gone. Two weeks! It looks like it's been vacant for a month. Look at the pile of junk on the dining room table!"

Martin ignored the table and wandered absently into the living room. He sat in his recliner relaxing back until the chair swallowed him up. "He's your son too, Birdie," his voice sounded from the depths of the upholstery.

Birdie mumbled as she sorted the mail on the table into piles. "Junk, junk, magazine, junk. Good grief, they're out early with this fall edition!" She flipped through the magazine glancing at the pictures, and then tossed it aside and looked around the living room.

Her eyes lit on a pair of marble ginger jars on the mantel above the fireplace. "Those are new." She started toward them for a closer look when a key scraped in the front door lock.

Sam walked into the entryway and froze. His eyes locked on Birdie's, and his jaw dropped nearly to his chest.

"What the hell are you staring at?"

"Ma ... Ma ... Mom?" Sam stuttered, barely breathing.

"No, Taylor Swift. Of course Mom! We're home. I told you we'd be home today. Didn't you notice the suitcases?" She pointed vaguely into the entryway.

Sam looked at the empty space. His mouth worked up and down, but no sound came out.

"Oh, for Pete's sake, your father must have rolled them into the bedroom. *Martin!*" she called.

"I'm right here Birdie." His voice echoed from deep in the recliner.

"And what are those *plants* doing in my entryway?" She pointed to the two humongous peace lilies.

Sam stared at her.

"Was that a hard question? You should know *something* about them, since you've supposedly been looking after the house."

Sam swallowed. "I was going to put them out with the trash Friday."

"Why wait! Drag those puppies out to the curb."

"I – I didn't want the neighbors to see."

"Why the hell not?"

"Because they gave them to us. You. Us." He swallowed again.

It was Birdie's turn to stare. "You really shouldn't drink in the middle of the week."

She looked him up and down. Sam was a fit young man, of medium height and build. He had been a competitive swimmer in college, and his body still bore the hallmarks. He had his father's dark brown hair, and the same kind eyes.

"I notice you got a haircut. I told you it would look nice shorter. See? You should listen to me once in a while."

Birdie seemed to remember something. "Did you interview for that job? I had it all set up for you."

"I didn't get that job, Ma. I'm still at the food bank."

"Oh, Samuel." She crossed her arms over her chest and clicked her tongue. "All that education, and can the boy get a real job? Is it so much to ask?"

"Ma, if you understood how many people we help." Sam's voice rose. "It's over ten percent of the population! Twenty counties!" His voice tapered off. "And you're not listening."

She shook her head and turned toward the living room again. "So what's with the big ginger jars? Is that a gift from the neighbors too? I never thought about ginger jars on the mantle, but they look pretty good. I bet those things weigh a ton." She walked closer to get a better look.

Sam took a step into the living room and shouted, "*Ma!*"

Birdie jumped with a shriek. "What the hell is wrong with you?"

"They – they're not ginger jars. They're *urns*." He stared at her with wide, soulful eyes.

She blinked back at him, then continued toward the fireplace. "Jars, urns, who the hell cares?"

She tilted her head back to look through the bottom of her bifocals, and leaned in closer to read a brass label on the jar on the right. "Martin E. Ebersole. What is this, like a trophy or something?" She mumbled as she continued reading, and then stopped.

"Oh, no. *Martin?*" Birdie began to shake.

"I'm right here Birdie." His voice echoed again from the recliner.

Sam stared at the carpet, his arms hanging at his sides. Birdie moved stiffly to the other urn and tilted her head back to read the label. "Brenda J. Ebersole ... Is this some kind of joke or something? Because it's not funny! Who would do something like this? With dates and everything. Is this a Halloween prank or something?"

"I wish it were a joke," Sam said to the carpet.

Birdie's voice quavered. "Oh, I have to sit down." She stumbled to the dining room table and dropped into one of the chairs, shoving junk mail out of her way. "Come and sit with your mother and tell me how this happened. Are you dead too? Is that why you got a haircut? Did the undertaker do that to you?"

"No, Ma, I got a haircut for the funeral. It's been three weeks ago now. It's growing out, but ... I did it for you."

He fiddled nervously with a stack of flyers on the table, and took a deep breath. "If you want to know, the bus you and Dad were on went into the river when the Midway Bridge collapsed."

"I always said that bridge wasn't safe," Martin said from his recliner.

"Someone shot a video from the east bank as it happened." Sam shuddered. "I've watched it a million times. It was all in the news. Everyone onboard was swept away and drowned." A tear slid down his face. He brushed it away with the back of his hand.

"Drowned." Birdie looked past him, gazing out the window. Splashes of vivid blue shone between the branches of the trees, but fall was coming on fast and the leaves had started turning amber and crimson. The wind tugged some of them free, and they twirled to the ground.

"I don't remember." Birdie paused. "I remember the trip was good. Your father and I, we had a nice time, a lot of laughs. And those bus seats were comfortable! I must have been asleep."

She reached out and patted her son's hand. "And you're not dead, so there's still hope. There are other jobs. I'm sure if I talk to your uncle ..."

"*Ma!* Don't talk to anybody about jobs for me, okay? For one thing, you're dead! You'll give someone a heart attack. And for another thing, I'm happy where I am. I'm paying my bills; it's all good. You don't have to worry about me. Don't you start with the tears! I've had enough of tears lately." He picked up a flyer and twisted it in his hands.

Birdie sniffed and cast a resentful glance at Sam. "How can a mother stop worrying about her only son? How? I only want to see you settled."

"I'm settled! I have a nice apartment, a pickup truck, friends."

"Pfft! Such friends!"

"And we're doing important work at the food bank."

"Food bank! You should be at a *real* bank, with your education. Then maybe you'd earn enough to pay off those college loans. Have you thought about that Mr. Smarty-Pants? Do you have that figured out?"

Sam stared at his hands as he twisted the flyer into a tight tube.

"Let me see that." Birdie snatched the paper and read it, then looked at the stack of identical flyers on the table. She raised her hands with a cry of disbelief. "You're selling my house!"

"What did you expect me to do with it? Turn it into a museum and sell tickets?"

"This is a beautiful house! It's a wonderful neighborhood. You used to love it here. It's a great place to raise kids."

"I don't have kids," Sam reminded her.

Birdie narrowed her eyes at him. "I wonder how long I can haunt you."

Chapter 2

"That man was here again."

Sam groaned. Of course his mother was still here, he thought. He had let himself into the house and paused in the entryway to listen. Everything was still, except for the electric clock in the dining room ticking out the seconds. Why an electric clock needed to make a ticking sound he didn't understand. He wished the battery would run out already. He listened another moment. That's when he heard his mother's disembodied voice.

"I said, that man was here again." She materialized, still wearing her purple outfit. "Am I talking to myself? Can anyone hear me? Earth to Samuel; come in Samuel."

He swallowed down the lump he felt every time he thought of his mother dead. He wished his parents were still alive. Everyone would be happier, and he wouldn't have to come over to the house on Fairlawn Street so often.

"I hear you, Ma. What man was here again?" Sam turned his back on her and switched on a couple of lamps in the living room.

The house felt cold, even though he wore thick socks and his favorite sweatshirt with the USA swimming logo. It didn't help that his hair was still damp from swimming at the rec center. He rubbed the back of his neck.

"The man who *calls* himself a realtor." Birdie folded her arms across her chest. "That man has the personality of a dead fish. No one's going to buy anything from him. I wouldn't buy a bottle of water from him if I were on fire."

"Bob's not a bad realtor, Ma." Sam wasn't sure why he felt compelled to defend the realtor. He'd only hired the guy because he was the friend of a friend, and truth to tell, Sam wasn't impressed either. "It's always hard to sell at this time of year. No one wants to pull their kids out of school once the schoolyear has started. Besides, the interest rates are killing us. They're up three points in the last three months. Nothing is selling right now. We might have to drop the price again."

"Drop the price?" Birdie raised her hands and looked at the ceiling. "He's giving my house away. Did you hear that, Martin?"

"Yes, I heard," Martin's voice echoed from deep in the recliner. "Don't give the house away, Son."

Birdie faced Sam with her hands on her hips. "Everything your father and I worked for. It means nothing to you? Look at me when I talk to you!"

Sam didn't answer. He gazed at the realtor's cards arrayed on the dining room table, mechanically picking them up and putting them back down.

He *was* almost ready to give the house away. It wasn't a bad house. Everything in it was completely familiar. Too familiar. He'd spent over eighteen years in the house, plus the summers when he came home from college. Wasn't that enough? Nothing had changed in years, and he wanted to move on.

He took a deep breath, and trudged to the small third bedroom his parents used as an office. He dug into the filing cabinet, pulled out a thick folder, and sat in the bulky office chair in front of the desk.

He needed to organize their financial paperwork and track down some insurance documents. Luckily his parents had things pretty much in order.

Sam's brain settled into analytical mode, absorbing details, arranging papers into piles, making mental calculations, and jotting down a few notes.

Birdie spoke, and Sam jumped in his seat.

"It's a beautiful house, Sammy, in a nice neighborhood. Don't just give it away."

He laid his pencil down and cupped the palms of his hands over his eyelids. "Don't worry, Ma. Before I drop the price I'll probably ask someone to help me stage it.

Make it look a little more presentable. Then maybe buyers will be more interested."

Birdie's eyes narrowed and she crossed her arms again. "Like put a – a bowl of lemons on the kitchen counter, and some stupid 'live-laugh-love' sign in the foyer? You think that's going to make a difference?" She drifted upwards on an invisible current, shaking her head. "I don't understand people. This place looks good like it is. It looks like home, like someplace you could move right in and put your feet up. But whatever!" She lifted her hands in a theatrical shrug, and turned away. "You're a grown man. Do what you think is best." She mumbled something about "breaking your mother's heart" as she faded into the ceiling.

Chapter 3

"Who is this person and why is she wandering all over my house?" Birdie whispered, as if anyone besides Sam could hear her. So far no one had. At least, not that he knew of. She watched nervously as a young woman took in the living room, the dining room, and the kitchen.

"This is Dee. She's going to help me stage the house," Sam said in a low voice.

"'D'? That's not a name, it's a letter. If she were a grade she'd barely be passing." Birdie followed a few steps behind her. "Where is she going now? That's my bedroom back there!"

"Dee. D-E-E." Sam spelled it out. "It's short for Deirdre. And you don't have to follow her."

"Deirdre. What the hell kind of a name is Deirdre?"

"It's a good name, Ma." He wished his mother would stop talking. "She's going to help rearrange a few things so we don't have to drop the price on the house."

A toilet flushed from the direction of the master suite. "Who are you talking to?" Dee asked, walking back into the living room. "Hey, we need to bring some more toilet paper. I hate it when I have to *go*, and there's no paper."

"Oh for cripe's sake." Birdie rolled her eyes.

Dee sank into the sofa across from Martin's recliner, and tucked her long sweater around herself.

"Oh sure. Make yourself at home," Birdie said under her breath. "Where did you find this bimbo? She looks like she needs a nap."

"Make yourself at home Sammy. Take a load off, and let's talk about this."

"*You're* inviting *him*? He used to live here, you know. Did you bother to tell her that, Samuel?"

Birdie hovered beside her husband's recliner and glared at Dee. "This girl looks familiar. Who does she remind you of, Martin?"

Martin remained silent. Sam watched warily as Birdie stepped closer and leaned over Dee, who raised her hand to brush away a lock of dark-brown hair that had fallen across her face. She closed her gray eyes and yawned, slouching down into the cushions. "This couch is comfortable. I think I might take a nap."

"Oh, no," Birdie said. "I know who this is. It's one of Colleen's girls. Look, Martin. Don't you think she's one of the Malloy kids from down the street?"

"Why don't you ask her, Birdie?" Martin answered.

"You know the ones I'm talking about! Their front yard always looked like a tornado hit it. The whole family was nothing but chaos. I think this was the last one, the *surprise* baby. The one who ran around in mismatched socks and hand-me-down clothes rescuing baby birds, or stray cats, or whatever it was. Lord, I haven't seen any of that bunch in years. Not since the mill shut down and John Malloy and all the rest who worked there got transferred. This girl couldn't have been much out of elementary school when that happened. What's she even doing back here?"

Birdie looked at Sam, who sat with a pained expression at the other end of the sofa struggling to ignore his mother. "What do you think, Dee?" he said. "What do we need to do to make this place a little more presentable?"

Dee opened her eyes and shifted on the couch, reaching out to take Sam's hand. Sam stroked the back of her hand with his thumb.

Birdie went ballistic.

"Oh, my God! What the hell is this? Samuel, this is *not* just some 'stager' you found. Is *this* the woman you started running around with? Because I know you were seeing someone. Right before we went on that vacation I said to your father that you hadn't been spending much time with us. You couldn't tell your poor old mother?"

"What do you think, huh?" Sam repeated, trying to drown his mother out.

"Let's take another look at the kitchen." Dee heaved herself off of the deep couch and led the way.

"Are you serious about this girl?" Birdie hissed, taking Dee's place on the couch. Sam growled softly at his mother, and followed Dee to the kitchen.

"Talk some sense into your son, Martin." Birdie rose from the couch and paced around the living room, pausing once at the mantle over the fireplace. Her eye fell on the urns that held hers and Martin's ashes. She clucked her tongue and turned to stare out the front window.

A hollow chuckle came from deep in the recliner. "I remember that kid. DeeDee, that's what they called her. A gutsy little thing. She was all over the neighborhood on that red bicycle."

"We used to have names for girls who were 'all over the neighborhood'," Birdie said. "Samuel can do better than that."

"Leave the boy alone, Birdie." Martin's voice sounded like it was coming from the bottom of a well. "I tried to talk him into joining me at the sewage plant, and you know how well that worked out. He's going to do what he wants to do. He's always been that way."

"Yes, but a mistake like this could ruin his whole life."

In the kitchen Dee struggled with the curtains behind the breakfast nook. "There's a nice view of the back yard from this window here. Look how much light comes in. Buyers love natural light in a kitchen. If we removed these old drapes and just left the blinds, it would look bigger."

"Hang on. There's a step ladder in the garage," Sam said, happy to have something practical to do. He came back and started pulling down the curtains.

"And the walls. They're not banged up or anything, but the color is just not doing it for me. I mean, wasn't this the 'color of the year' in 1998?"

"Hey, ninety-eight was a good year," Sam said. It happened to be the year he was born.

"You're so old!" Dee, who was only slightly younger, never missed a chance to tease him, especially when she found a white hair on his prematurely graying head.

"Have you thought about getting rid of all the stuff in the cabinets and drawers? Anyone who buys this place is likely to have their own dishes and silverware, you know." She opened one of the cupboards. "I kind of like this sage-green cabinetry. You could change the hardware to make it look a little more contemporary. And it would really pop if the walls were painted a soft cream."

"Changing hardware is one thing, but painting? I wasn't planning to put that kind of time into the place."

"Hey, you asked my opinion. I'm just telling you what you could do to make it look nicer. You know, your realtor should have told you this stuff. Where did you find that guy?"

Sam shrugged. He was tired of defending Bob the realtor. "He said houses show better with furniture and stuff in them. It makes it easier for people to imagine them with – furniture and stuff ..." He trailed off, feeling silly.

Dee grunted. "Granted I only met him once, but he has all the personality of a dead fish. It's no wonder you haven't had any decent offers yet. I wouldn't buy a bottle of water from him if I were on fire."

Sam froze. "What did you say?"

"I said, I wouldn't buy a bottle of water from that guy if I were on fire. Hey, come here, and take a look now."

The curtains were down and Dee waved Sam into the middle of the kitchen. He placed his hands on his hips as he gazed out the window. "Wow," he said. "You were right. It does open the room up. Those mature trees should make the place worth a few thousand more, I think."

"I love those trees. I bet this yard is nice and shady in the summer." Dee reached for his hand again. "Let's take another look at the master suite. That's the other place that will make or break it for a buyer. I can tell you already, the carpet in that bathroom has got to go!"

Holding hands, they passed through the living room. Sam forced himself to look straight ahead, and not at his mother who stood near the dining room windows.

"So," Dee said in a business-like tone looking around the master bathroom. "Pull out this bathroom carpet, like I said. Who knows what's under it. Maybe it's that same tile like we had in my parents' old house. The rest of the bathroom just needs a coat of paint."

She turned to survey the bedroom. "His and hers closets. They're not big enough, but what else is new? Here again, I say get rid of these old drapes so people can actually see the windows." She pushed the drapes aside as far as they would go. "And picture this room in a soft dove gray. It would be nice, actually, and so peaceful."

Dee looked thoughtful. "We never looked at the other two bedrooms. Let's check them out." She walked back through the living room to the other side of the house, sighing when she passed the second bathroom. "Maybe you can just say it's retro. At least it's clean. Tell me about these other rooms."

"My parents always used this room as an office," Sam said indicating the first.

Dee glanced inside and nodded. "That's a nice feature," she said. "Lots of people work from home these days."

"And this room next to it was mine."

"Oh, my God." Dee placed a hand over her mouth and turned slowly, taking everything in — the books in Sam's bookcase, the scout memorabilia, the trophies he won on the swim team. "What is this, like a shrine? I mean, this is all your stuff, right?"

"Ma asked me to go through it. I just haven't had time. Most of it's junk." Sam looked around at the bed, the dresser, and other furniture he'd had for nearly two decades. He picked up a light saber from a shelf over his old desk and swished it back and forth while Dee checked out the bobble-heads on top of the bookcase.

"These are so cute! It kind-of looks like you moved out when you were ten years old." She smiled. "I wouldn't put any time into this room, other than boxing up your old stuff. At least that way people could see the room, instead of all your *treasures*." She walked to the window to look out, and then turned. "Let's go back to the living room. My feet are tired."

"Why don't you stretch out on the couch," Sam suggested, "and I'll go through this stuff. There are some cardboard boxes out in the garage."

"I like that idea." Dee headed back to the living room while Sam fetched a box and got to work.

Chapter 4

"Why couldn't it be that pretty girl he dated when he was in college?" Birdie asked Martin. She paced the living room darting glances at Dee, who lay stretched out on the sofa with her eyes closed and her sweater pulled tight around her.

"Now *she* was a *looker*," Martin said. "Amber, her name was. Just gorgeous." A wolf-whistle sounded from the re-cliner.

Birdie tutted. It was okay for her to notice pretty girls, but she didn't like Martin to act so enthusiastic. "Maybe she was a little too made-up," she said with a sniff.

"I don't know why that girl hung around with Samuel. I knew that couldn't last. This Dee is cute, though. She has good hair."

Birdie snorted. "Yeah, she's cute if you like the freck-led, outdoorsy type." Birdie never freckled. She rarely even spent enough time outdoors to get a tan.

She leaned over Dee, who slept soundly. Despite the scattering of freckles on her nose, the young woman's cheeks had a soft rosiness, and her hair fell in glossy waves around her face. Birdie had to admit it. Dee was not gorgeous, but she was definitely attractive. Pretty, even.

"What's that son of ours doing now?" Birdie said. "I saw him carrying a box. He's probably getting rid of our family heirlooms. I wish I could hide mother's silverware."

She found Sam going through old clothes he had left in the closet. He kept a couple of things to wear if he got around to painting the rooms Dee had suggested, and carefully folded the rest.

"I always thought there would be time for us to deal with this." Birdie waved a hand, taking in his room and the house in general. "Sorry I didn't give you any siblings to help out with everything."

Sam was silent for a moment. "It's okay, Ma. No one expected ... I mean, I'm sorry you're not..." Sam shrugged, and dropped a stack of clothes into the box. He wondered if it was polite to talk to a ghost about being dead. "We had some fun, our family."

"I loved being your mom," she told him, the words surprising her. "I just wish I had been around for more of your childhood. I was working all the time, and you were in daycare, school, summer day camp...."

"You were a den mother when I was in cub scouts, I remember that. And you were at all my swim meets. We took those trips to the beach or the mountains every year with my cousins, and back and forth to Grandma's house. It was good, Ma. It was good."

"I used to feel guilty that I wasn't here when you got home from school. I always tried to organize my day so that I could shoot out of that place at five o'clock, and damn if something wouldn't come up to make me late, or traffic would be insane. I wish I'd been there for you."

"Don't beat yourself up about it, Ma. I didn't turn out that bad, did I?"

"But you must have been lonely every afternoon, here by yourself."

"Are you kidding? There were so many kids in this neighborhood, I had to *work* to be lonely. I'd hang out with Steve across the street, or with Jack and Charlie down at the Malloy's house. There was always something going on down there, and Mrs. Malloy or Maureen or Trish always had snacks for us. I'd spend afternoons there, and just come back here when it was time for you or Dad to get home."

"I forgot all their names. Trish was the oldest, wasn't she? I think she even babysat you a few times."

"No, that was Maureen. She's the oldest. Then Trish, then Charlie, and then Jack who was my age, give or take. Then Dee was born three years later."

Birdie tried to ignore the pang in the area where her heart used to be. She hated to admit that she was jealous of anyone like Colleen Malloy. Colleen, who didn't work a paying job, but stayed home with her brood of wild and beautiful children.

"What's Dee doing back in town?" Birdie asked.

"Sharing an apartment with Trish. Trish and Maureen both work at the hospital. Maureen's married. All three girls are moved back here. Charlie and Jack are in Colorado."

"I suppose Dee has a job somewhere? What does she do for a living?" Birdie asked.

"She works in the office at Walsh Windows and Doors. Her uncle owns the place. It's a good job for now. Dee takes care of the web page, online advertising, social media, and all that, plus she does freelance web design and marketing on the side. She's really brilliant at that stuff. I was looking for a freelancer to redo the web page for the food bank, and someone mentioned her. That's how I learned she was back in town."

A good job for now. Birdie wondered what that meant. She had loved her job. She was included in all the important meetings with the company executives just like one of the guys, making sure the presentations were all up to snuff, taking notes on all the big decisions, handling important paperwork. Her boss loved her. She never would have retired if it wasn't for Martin's health scare.

And hadn't she been brilliant at using all of the office programs? Not to mention she was the only one who could ever get the printers straightened out when there was a paper jam. As for the other hardware, she sure had missed the help desk guys after she retired. A couple of grandkids would have come in handy, to help her figure out all those apps on her phone. It just hadn't been in the cards.

Sam's cellphone pinged, startling Birdie. She floated back to the living room, where the sofa was empty. She heard the toilet flush again, and found Dee in the master bedroom.

Dee peered out of the bedroom windows, humming a monotonous little tune. She looked around again, and touched the arm of the rocking chair, setting it moving back and forth.

Then she stood in front of the large mirror over the dresser and admired her reflection. She placed one hand at the top of her stomach and the other hand at the bottom, turning to the side with a pleased little smile at the slight bump that was now apparent.

Birdie gasped, her eyes round, and raised her hands in the air. *"Martin!"* she shrieked. "Wait until I tell him. I sure as hell hope she's told Samuel!" She whirled like a small tornado and dissolved in an angry puff of sparks.

Chapter 5

Dee padded through the living room pulling her sweater close. She passed the thermostat, tempted to turn it up, but decided against it since Sam had recently mentioned the utility bills.

She leaned against the door jamb of his bedroom and watched as he sorted through items in the top dresser drawer. She loved the look of him. She loved to run her fingers through the dark curls at the base of his neck, and to look into his warm brown eyes. "You know, Sammy, if we lived here we'd be home by now."

He tossed a couple of things into the nearby waste paper basket and looked up. "Sorry to take so long. I guess you're ready to leave." He gave a hopeless shrug, looking around. "It never seemed like the right time to empty this room out while my parents were still –" He was about to say *here*, but instead finished the sentence with "living."

Dee sat on the edge of the small bed and beckoned to Sam. He sat beside her and reached for her hand, weaving his fingers through hers. "I'm sorry I didn't get to spend any time with them. I can't imagine what life is going to be like when *my* parents are gone." She looked at him with love and sympathy in her gray eyes.

"Especially since we're expecting now." He placed a gentle hand on her belly. "Ma would have been over the moon."

"Too bad I was in denial for so long. Poor Sammy." Dee leaned into him and gave him a tender kiss.

He kissed her back, taking his time. He combed his fingers through her soft hair, and stroked her shoulders. Then he burrowed his chilly hands inside her sweater, holding her tight.

"I bet it's a lot warmer under the covers," Dee said with a playful tug at his shirttail.

Sam started to yield, and then froze. He had the uneasy feeling that his mother might appear in the room any minute. "This old bed is really uncomfortable," he said. He pulled his arms free to look at his watch. "Oh, gosh, look at the time. We both need to get to work tomorrow." He rose and took Dee's hands to pull her to her feet.

She regarded him with a bemused smile. "Like I said, if we lived here we'd be home now. And about that. Trish is after me to clear my stuff out of her apartment. But I haven't really wanted to drag everything up the stairs to your apartment."

"*Our* apartment," he interrupted.

"Whatever. But you know it has all those stairs, and only two bedrooms, and, well – like I've said …"

"I know. It's dark and ugly and too small." He ticked off the features of the apartment on his fingers.

"And they just told you they're raising the rent! You majored in business. You know it's not a good investment to be giving all that cash to someone else and getting nothing for it."

"Except a place to live," Sam pointed out.

"This *house* is a place to live!" Dee raised her eyebrows at Sam and waited for him to catch up.

"You mean, us move in here?"

Dee looked around his old bedroom. "Wouldn't this make a sweet nursery?"

"Why would I want to come back here?" The house was history, and he was ready to move on, to start a new chapter. To live his own life, different from his parents'.

It was Dee's turn to tick things off on her fingers. "The house hasn't sold in three months, which means it's been costing you money. It's a nice size for a starter home. It's in an established neighborhood with mature trees. It's decent commuting distance to our places of employment, not to mention that home office."

"Okay. Okay. But Dee, I've lived here since I was an infant!"

"The happiest years of my life were when I lived down the road in a house just like this one. At least, it was like this before my parents added on those extra bedrooms. I loved this neighborhood with all the kids, and everything close by. The library, the playground at the church, the city pool, that rinky-dink little corner store where Maureen used to buy me ice cream sandwiches. You just have to try to see the place with new eyes. Take the emotion out of it."

Sam laughed a mirthless laugh.

"Or, leave the emotion in. You told me you always liked this neighborhood, and this house. You said you had a great childhood."

"I didn't say great, I said good."

Dee tightened her grip on his hand and led him through the house again, room by room. She paused first at the office. "I would love a place like this where I could set up my monitors and work, and leave stuff out when I was done. Not like the dining table at Trish's apartment, where I have to pack everything up all the time."

They moved on. "I already told you, I like this kitchen and the view of the back yard. The living room and dining room flow together, which is great for parties and things. I know, you're such a party animal. We're going to have to work on that." Sam groaned.

Back in the master bedroom she said, "Now here's the room where you should be boxing things up." She pulled open a closet door where Birdie's belongings were still on hangers and shelves inside. Dee's voice turned more sympathetic. "It must be hard to get rid of these things. So let me help!"

"You can't tell, but I actually did go through some of it. I snagged a couple of Dad's neckties, and a cool winter hat I gave him one Christmas, the kind with the earflaps and the fur inside. His clothes don't fit me, though, even if they were my style."

Dee was thoughtful as she brushed her palm against the clothes in Birdie's closet. "Our mothers were so different. My mom always in corduroy pants or cut-off shorts. Your mom in chic slacks and cashmere, or some gauzy harem pants and a flowy blouse. I love my mother, but I idolized yours. How sharp she always looked coming home from work in those skirted suits, with her handbag matching her shoes. I wanted to be just like her, and have a job in some fancy office somewhere. You know, I came real close to dropping out of college a few times, but I would picture your mom and remember that dream I had, and put my shoulder back to the wheel."

She closed the closet door and sat on the bed. Sam stood in front of her and she reached for both his hands. "I have a feeling about this house, like I'm in *agreement* with it, or something. The place feels like home, like I just want to settle in and put my feet up. With a few tweaks and some new paint, we could move right in."

Sam pulled his hands free and slid them in his pockets. His dead parents were still in the house. How could he live here? Then again, how could he sell the place out from under them to someone else? He walked over to the window and stared at his reflection in the glass. The moonlight gave the trees in the backyard a subtle, eerie glow.

He turned to face Dee again, and rubbed the back of his neck where the tension had taken root. "I don't know, I just don't *know*." He sat beside her and whispered, "I feel like my parents are still here, in this house."

Dee cocked her head. "Well, it might help if you got their ashes off the mantel."

"It's not just that! I come to the house and *she's here*. My mother's here. Dad's here too."

Dee's eyes grew round. She pulled away slightly and stared at Sam. "You mean, like, *haunting the place?* Do you see them every time?" Her eyes darted back and forth and she lowered her voice. "Are they here now, listening to us?"

Sam shook his head.

"Do you think they have *unfinished business* or something?" She made air quotes. "There's no one buried in the back yard, is there?"

"Ma didn't realize she was dead. She figured it out from the urns, and from stumbling over the peace lilies."

"I hate those darn things. They make the house look like a funeral parlor, and they clutter up the entryway. I don't understand why you haven't got rid of them."

"She didn't tell you to say that, did she?" Sam let out a nervous laugh. "Ma hated the lilies too. But the neighbors sent them. Nice people. They always bought from me when the scouts were selling stuff." His voice trembled, and he looked down at his hands.

Dee elbowed him in the ribs and grinned. "Do you think that's why she's haunting you? Because of the peace lilies?" Sam's frown didn't budge.

She lifted his chin to look in his eyes. "Hey. You've been under a lot of pressure lately, trying to settle the estate and sell this house. Nothing says we have to make a decision tonight. We can come back and clear out the closets and cabinets, do a little painting and what-not. If the place sells right off after that, then we know it's not for us. But if it's still here, we can talk about it again."

Chapter 6

The following Saturday Dee turned the key in the lock and pushed the front door open. "Hello. Anybody home?" She took off her coat and hung it on the back of a dining room chair.

"Are you really expecting an answer?" Trish, a blue-eyed blonde, entered behind Dee with a stack of folded cardboard boxes.

"You never know. The realtor or someone might be here."

"Sam's just pulling in the drive," Maureen said. She pushed past her sisters with more boxes, and placed a large roll of packing tape on the dining room table. Then she shrugged out of her jacket and adjusted the bandana she wore over her auburn hair.

"So those are the peace lilies you told us about," Trish said. "They do kind-of take over the entryway. Do you want one Mo? Otherwise I'm going to dump them behind the shrubs at the side of the house when Sam isn't looking."

"Heck no," Mo said. "Dump away. I think they're creepy."

"Sammy'll probably let himself in through the garage with the paint," Dee said. "As soon as he comes in the back door you can sneak the lilies out the front." The garage door shrieked and rumbled at the other side of the house. "I'll head him off at the pass while you do the deed."

"Come on, Mo. I'll get one and you get the other." Trish picked up a pot and staggered to the door. "Oof! These suckers are heavy!"

Moments later the two walked into the kitchen a little out of breath to say hi to Sam.

"Thanks for helping us today," he said. "I should have emptied the place a long time ago."

"Happy to be here," Maureen said.

"We're practically family now," Trish added. "So take us around the house, DeeDee, and show us what needs to be packed up."

"The kitchen for sure," Dee said. "Sammy can start painting over by the windows while we pull things out of the cabinets. Come on. I'll show you around."

Sam spread newspapers on the kitchen table and fiddled with his paint tray and brushes while Dee walked her sisters through the rest of the house.

"You're painting the kitchen."

Sam was not surprised to hear his mother's voice. He looked up and saw her leaning against the sink. He pulled his phone out of his pocket and launched a playlist on his favorite streaming app. Mellow music filled the kitchen.

"Are you trying to drown me out?" Birdie asked.

"No, Ma," Sam said quietly. "I'm trying to drown myself out, so the girls don't think I've gone crazy. No one else can hear you, so they'll think I'm talking to myself."

"Oh." She moved closer and peered into the paint can. "That's a nice color. You're doing the walls, right? Not the cabinets?"

"Right. Apparently the cabinets are on trend the way they are, so we're just refreshing the walls and brightening things up."

"I love these green cabinets. I wanted them like this because it was the same color my grandma had. My mother thought I was nuts. She hated it, but that's what I wanted."

"Was that the grandma you got the apple cake recipe from?" It was his favorite, the one he asked for every birthday when he was growing up.

"That's the one. She was quite a woman, my grandma. We would talk for hours while she cooked or ironed."

Sam stirred the paint in the can around and around, although it didn't need mixing. He was waiting for the lump in his throat to dissolve. His child – children? – would never know their Grandma Birdie.

Dee and her sisters returned to the kitchen. Maureen taped together a cardboard box while the others opened drawers and cabinets. Birdie scowled at Dee, who looked more obviously pregnant today in her stretchy jeans and sweatshirt.

"Some of this is good stuff, you know," Birdie whispered to Sam, standing beside him near the windows. "Why don't you have a yard sale? Couldn't you use the extra money?"

"Yard sale?" Sam said aloud.

Maureen looked up curiously, and peered around the room. "Did you say something?" she asked Sam.

He cleared his throat. "I said 'yard sale.' Someone suggested we have a yard sale. Maybe make some money from all this stuff."

Trish gave a dismissive snort. "When was the last time *you* had a yard sale?" she asked. "They're a whole lot of work, everyone expects you to *give* your things away, and you still have tons of stuff to cart to Goodwill when it's all over. I say we cut to the chase. Just box it all up and donate it from the get-go."

"Some of this is good stuff, though," Dee said. Sam paused with his brush in mid-air.

"Although you'd probably have to *pay* someone to take these." Dee grabbed a handful of old wooden spoons and egg-turners out of a crock beside the stove and tossed them into the box.

"Of course some things are well-used!" Birdie said, crossing her arms over her chest. "I'm no Martha Stewart, but I did cook once in a while."

"They're definitely well-used," Dee said. "But even Martha Stewart probably has a favorite wooden spoon that she's worn down to a nub."

Sam stopped painting as his heart skipped a beat. He glanced sideways at Dee, wondering if she could hear his mother, and just hadn't told him.

Her sisters made short work of packing away the cookware. Dee pulled open a drawer full of silverware and slowly looked it over.

She barely owned the basics when it came to tableware, since she'd never had a place of her own. Her college roommates had come well-supplied, and Dee was only out of college a short while. Trish had everything she wanted in her kitchen. As long as Dee had been living with her sister she didn't see the need to acquire much else. Sammy had the basics also. But not the things Birdie had assembled over the years. This silverware was beautiful.

And what if she and Sammy did stay in the house? It would be a shame to give all this away only to have to buy it again.

"I'd like to keep this silverware, if you don't mind," Dee said, glancing up.

Sam stood a couple of steps up the ladder to cut in fresh paint above the window frame. "Sure. You and your sisters, take whatever you want." He scanned the kitchen and glanced at his mother who stood at the base of the ladder.

An image from a poltergeist movie flashed through his mind. He wondered briefly if there were knives in the drawer Dee was working on, and clung more tightly to the ladder. Then he relaxed his grip. His mother sometimes had a wicked tongue, but he'd never seen her get violent. Not while she was alive, at least.

Birdie let out a big sigh, and then threw her hands up in an elaborate shrug. "Okay, fine. Clear it all out. Who the hell cares anymore."

Maureen took a step backward, looking toward the window. The sun caused a hazy aura around Sam and the ladder, but she thought there was something more. She turned her back to open a cupboard full of glasses and mugs, but felt a prickle between her shoulder blades, as if someone were close behind her.

Finally she said, "Dee I think you and Trish can finish in here. Why don't I get started on those master closets?"

"Good idea. We'll join you in a bit," Dee said.

Maureen glanced once more toward the window, and then hurried from the kitchen.

Chapter 7

Maureen carried an empty box through the living room, and paused in front of a recliner placed with a good view of the television. A shadow fell across it, and briefly Maureen thought she saw someone sitting there, but decided it must be the afghan laid over the back. Crossing herself, she picked up the pace as she passed by the mantel where the urns full of ashes stood.

Birdie followed, a misty shadow gliding along the edges of the ceiling. A whiffling snore rose from the upholstery on the recliner. How could Martin sleep when strangers were in their house, pawing through their things? The kitchen was one thing, but their bedroom? There were some personal items in there.

There was plenty of natural light in the master bedroom, but Maureen switched on the overhead fixture anyway, and cracked open a window to let in some fresh air. The room felt oppressive. The whole house did, actually.

She was a little sorry that she had volunteered to spend her Saturday helping her sister empty it. But many hands made light work, and sooner begun is sooner done, as their mom would say. She hated the thought that someday she might be doing this in her own parents' house.

She opened the door on the first closet, yanked on the pull chain to light the ceiling light and pulled out several pair of men's shoes, dropping them in the cardboard box for donations.

Next she folded pants and suits and boxed them, saving the nice wooden hangers. Shirts and other items she piled into the box, hangers and all.

She dragged the full box to the front hallway, and went to the kitchen to fetch another. "Oh, I like that color on the walls. It's looking good." She surveyed the kitchen with hands on hips before grabbing another cardboard box and taping the bottom. "DeeDee should you really be up on a ladder?"

Sam ducked his head shielding it with one arm. "Uh-oh. She said the next person who asked her that was going to get clubbed with a meat mallet."

"For the third time, it's not a ladder, it's a step stool," Dee huffed. "And I'm only on the first step. I'll be *fine*." She carried on wiping out the inside of a cupboard. "I'm just wiping off the lower shelves, for when people look inside. Who knows why, but people always open the cupboards. What are they expecting to find?"

"Ooh, wouldn't it be fun to put in a booby-trap, like one of those springy snakes that pops out of a can?" Trish said from under the kitchen sink.

Maureen snickered. "You two work on that. I'm going to empty another closet."

She returned to the master and shivered. The room was getting colder. She closed the window, opened the second closet and knelt on the floor.

Here the shoes were in boxes. She pulled the lid off one to find a stylish pair of navy leather heels. She bent one of the shoes expecting the sole to crack, but it was still in good shape. She checked the size number on the box.

Curious, she pulled off her right tennis shoe and her sock, and slipped on the pump. She didn't dress up much, but when she did she often wore navy. It set off her fair skin and her auburn hair. A pair of nice pumps might come in handy.

There was a sliding whoosh behind her, and cold air chilled the back of her neck. The window she had just closed had sprung open again.

Maureen peered around the room, and closed the window with a shiver. Then she sat on the end of the bed to pull off her left shoe and sock, and slipped on the other pump. The shoes were comfortable, slightly broken in but still looking great. She stood up and bent forward to admire her feet. Suddenly she felt a push from behind, and toppled onto the carpet.

Maureen rolled onto her back and stared at the ceiling, her heart pounding. She dug her heels into the carpet to slip the pumps off her feet, and crab-walked backwards out the door of the bedroom. When she reached the hallway she stood and ran barefoot back to the kitchen.

Trish looked up from under the kitchen sink where she was still emptying out cleaning supplies and saw Maureen's wide eyes and paler-than-usual face. "Maureen, what is it? What's the matter?"

"You guys, this place is…" She swallowed, looking at Sam. "It's haunted."

Chapter 8

Sam hung his head with a sigh, nearly smearing paint in his hair.

Trish looked from her sister to Sam and back again. "Maureen, are you sure?"

"What do you mean, haunted?" Dee exclaimed. "This house is perfectly fine. I *love* this house. How can it be haunted?"

"DeeDee, I know what I'm talking about. I can feel someone. I'm pretty sure it's the ghost of a woman. And there might be more than one."

"Mo, for heaven's sake, since when can you *feel ghosts?*" Dee asked.

Maureen and Trish looked at each other. "Mo has been sensitive to things like that for a long time," Trish said.

"What?" Dee's voice was several pitches higher than normal. "My sister is a psychic, and nobody ever told me? What else don't I know about my own family?"

Maureen shrugged, shaking her head. "Trust me. It's not like it's a special gift, or anything. It's actually a pain. I've been running from ghosts half my life."

"Since when?"

"You remember when mom and dad pulled me out of St. Luke's school and sent me to the public school?"

"Not really, since I was maybe in kindergarten at the time. Are you telling me St. Luke's was haunted?" Dee asked, incredulous.

Trish and Maureen both nodded. "Wait. Trish, do you see them too?"

Trish quickly shook her head.

"I don't always *see* them," Maureen corrected. "I can sense something, and I know they're there. And it's like there's someone talking but it's too faint to hear. Or – or I get that feeling someone is looking at me." She shivered. "Although this ghost is a little *pushier* than most."

Dee looked slowly around the kitchen. "Is someone in here now?"

"No. Not now. It – she – was in the bedroom. I think she was mad because I tried on a pair of her shoes."

Dee groped behind her for the stool and eased herself down. "This is crazy. Sammy, you lived here. Do you know anything about this?" She desperately hoped he could explain everything rationally and make it all better.

Sam looked sheepish, and sighed. "Maureen is right. I tried to tell you, remember? I told you they were still in the house."

"*They?* What do you mean, they? Do you know these ghosts?"

"They're my parents! I told you it felt like my parents were still in the house."

"Oh, jeez, I thought that was just a figure of speech!" Dee closed her eyes. She laced her fingers and clamped her hands over her head, trying to put her blown mind back together.

"Have you always had this – problem too?" Maureen asked Sam.

He laughed nervously. "I've *never* had this happen before. I hope it's not the start of something."

"There must be a reason why it's happening now. Does anyone know?" Dee asked. "It's not like they died *here* or anything. Do your parents just not want us here?"

Sam shrugged. "Ma keeps telling me what a great house this is."

Dee put her brave face on. "Well, I don't intend to be scared away by a ghost. I mean, the person least likely to hurt you is someone who's *already dead,* right? So, Madam Psychic." She addressed Maureen. "Tell us what we have to do. It's nothing personal, Sam, but how do we get your parents to leave?"

Maureen's eyes widened. "I've never been asked that before. I usually try to keep my distance from ghosts. I don't seek them out, and I definitely don't pick fights with them."

"Maybe we can call the rectory at St. Luke's, and ask Father Mike to do an exorcism," Trish suggested.

"Wait a minute." Sam sounded anxious. "These are my parents we're talking about. Isn't exorcism to get rid of the devil or some kind of evil spirit?"

"Right," Maureen agreed. "I think exorcism is something they do to expel demons. Your mom may have been mad at me for trying on her shoes without permission, but that's not the same as demonic possession. Besides, Father Mike probably couldn't do it. It would have to be a bishop or – or an exorcist, or something."

Dee wrapped her arms around herself and moaned. "You guys are creeping me out."

"Don't worry, Dee." Sam came to stand beside her and placed a hand around her shoulder. "We're not talking about evil demonic powers here. We're talking about my mom. You always admired my mom, remember?"

"Maybe there's some kind of blessing for the house." Dee said. "Or maybe a cleansing ritual. Think, you guys! My brain is a little frazzled right now."

"*Your* brain is frazzled!" Maureen said. "I'm the one who was just knocked over by a ghost. And by the way, my feet are getting cold. Who wants to go with me into the bedroom to get my shoes and socks?"

"I'll go," Sam said. "My mother doesn't scare me. At least, no more than she always did."

The two left the room, and Dee mechanically resumed packing pot holders and dish towels. "This is not good. I don't think we can very well sell a haunted house, let alone consider living here."

Trish clicked her tongue. "It's not like you're in a poltergeist movie and ghosts are trying to kill you or something."

"You heard Maureen. A ghost pushed her! I don't want some ectoplasmic *thing* assaulting me. Not in my condition." Dee placed a hand protectively over her belly. A tear blossomed at the edge of her eyelashes and rolled down her cheek.

"Don't worry," Trish said. "Between Maureen and Sam and me, we'll figure something out."

Chapter 9

Sam walked through the house with Maureen following closely behind.

"I don't see anyone in the living room," he said.

"I'm right here, Son," an echoey voice rose from Martin's chair.

"I take that back," Sam said, pointing.

Maureen placed her hand over her mouth. "What do you know. A haunted recliner. I'm glad I didn't try to sit there."

"Hey! What happened to the peace lilies in the entry way?" Sam asked.

"Peace lilies? I didn't see any peace lilies." Maureen shrugged her shoulders trying to look innocent.

Sam felt a stab of grief. He had grown weirdly attached to those plants. They were a living reminder of his parents, and now they were gone. He glanced back at the recliner and realized the absurdity of the thought.

"Don't be mad," Maureen said, "but Dee hated them, so Trish and I dumped them outside. Besides, they're toxic to cats."

"We don't have a cat." He stared blankly at her.

"You don't have a cat *yet*. Seriously, how well do you know DeeDee? Are you sure you two should be moving in together?"

"I've known Dee half her life. I was crushing on Dee since before your family moved away to Newburgh," Sam said.

Maureen gave him an appraising look. "I must have missed all that. Where was I? High school maybe? Or no. Probably college."

"And anyway, no need to apologize about those plants. You probably just made one ghost very happy."

He stepped over the threshold into the bedroom and looked around. "The coast is clear. Get your shoes and socks. I'll have to finish packing up in this room."

"Sorry. At least I got your dad's closet cleared out. By the way, this is the plushest carpet. It feels really good, walking around in here."

"Yeah, my dad's into comfort. *Was* into comfort. His job kept him on his feet a lot. When he got home all he wanted to do was sit in his chair. Anyway, he got the extra-thick padding under the carpet in here. He's also the reason for the carpeting in the bathroom, which Dee hates."

Sam watched Maureen sit tentatively on the end of the bed to put on her socks. "So, you can sense my mom's ghost, and I can of course, but it seems like no one else can."

"Are you sure about that?" Maureen asked. "Are you sure the reason the house hasn't sold is just the market and the timing? Maybe your mom's been scaring off potential home buyers."

"I never thought …" Something nagged at the back of Sam's mind. "Do you know if Dee can sense ghosts too?"

Maureen looked thoughtful. "I don't know. My 'talent,' if you want to call it that, manifested when I hit puberty. I was mostly away from home when Dee was that age. My folks never said anything about Dee sensing ghosts, but then, apparently they didn't tell Dee about me either."

"I guess I thought my mom was just haunting *me*."

"It could be a combination of you *and* the house," Maureen guessed. "Maybe she's just not ready to leave. Not that I'm an expert at this stuff. In fact, it scares me. It's why I retrained to become a nurse nutritionist. There were too many people dying where I worked before. Helping people improve their diets is a lot less frightening for me."

"Well, maybe between the two of us we could, you know, convince my parents to move on and go wherever ghosts are supposed to go in the afterlife."

Maureen sighed wearily. "I really don't like messing with ghosts." Sam's face fell. "But, look. I know how much

DeeDee wants this house, so – we can try. You may have to do a lot of the talking, since my communications with your mom have been limited at best."

"Thanks, Mo. Let's go tell your sisters."

Chapter 10

"Let me get this straight. We're going to have a reverse séance, and instead of just summoning the spirits, you're going to tell them to go away?" Dee fished the last french fry out of the little paper bag. She sat between her sisters on the sofa finishing the fast-food Trish had picked up from the local Wendy's. Sam stood next to the fireplace slowly eating spoonfuls of his chocolate Frosty.

"That's right," Maureen said, scooping up the last few shredded carrots from her salad bowl. "A reverse séance."

"And you've done this before?"

"Oh, dozens of times. I just order the do-it-yourself séance kit online!" She smirked at Dee, waving her fork in the air. "Look, baby sis, I'm trying this for you. The least you can do is act positive."

"Okay, okay, settle down. *When* can we do it? I'm ready to get this show on the road." Dee clasped her hands in her lap and patiently waited to hear the plan.

Sam interrupted. "You know, I could just try asking my parents to vacate." He faced the recliner and spoke a little louder. "They did leave the house and everything to me in the will. There wasn't any clause that said they could continue living here. And anyway, those are usually only good while the people named in the clause are alive."

"So tell them to go, Sammy." Dee looked at him expectantly.

Sam cleared his throat. "Ahem. Ma? Dad?" He waited. "Dad, are you there?" He walked over and nudged the recliner.

"Maybe they know they aren't wanted, and decided to leave," Trish said.

A soft snoring sound came from the recliner. "I don't think so," Sam said.

Maureen shivered. "I don't think so either. Look over toward the foyer. Is that just light coming through the sidelight, or is that a ... You know, an apparition?"

Dee squinted toward the front door. "I don't see anything."

"I'm glad you finally got rid of the dumb plants," Birdie said sulkily from the entryway. "It only took you, what, six months?"

"Not that long, Ma."

"Who is he talking to?" Trish asked.

Dee shook her head. "Hey, I just noticed! Look how much nicer the foyer looks without those dumb plants. Thanks, guys!" She patted Trish and Maureen on the knee.

Sam's eyes widened.

"You told her to say that, didn't you," Birdie said.

"I didn't tell her anything," Sam replied. "Can you hear her, Dee?"

"Hear what?"

Trish gave a sideways glance at Sam as she stood to gather up hamburger wrappers. "It's like listening to one side of a phone conversation."

"Shhh!" Maureen said.

The four of them grew still and listened to the quiet. A car drove by outside. The furnace blower kicked on somewhere in the house.

Dee shrugged. "All I hear is the heater coming on."

Sam took a deep breath and addressed the foyer. "Ma, have you been listening? You really shouldn't be here anymore. I told you what happened with your bus on the bridge. It's time for you and Dad to move on to ... whatever comes next. You and Dad were good people, so I'm sure there's something nice waiting for you, probably."

Trish snickered. "'*Probably?*' If I were your mother I would definitely haunt you for that!"

"I'm not going anywhere until we talk things over and straighten things out," Birdie said. She folded her arms with a stubborn air.

"Okay. What things do we need to straighten out?" Sam asked, trying to remain patient.

"I want to know what your plans are with …" She pointed toward Dee on the sofa.

"Dee? What about her?"

"What about me?" Dee asked.

"It's not just a her, it's a *them!*" Birdie said.

Maureen got off the sofa. "I don't like the vibes I'm getting. I can't hear what she's saying, but I take it you haven't convinced your parents to go, so I think it's time for *me* to leave. I told Ryan I'd only be gone for a couple of hours anyway. Come on, Trish."

"Wait! We haven't decided when to do the séance," Dee said.

Maureen sighed. "I can probably get away tomorrow evening, as long as it's not too late. I need to make sure the kids get in bed early for school Monday."

"You want to say around six then? Is that too early?"

"Six-thirty. And you all need to be here to back me up, in case things start going crazy. Or in case *I* go crazy," she added.

"Six-thirty it is. And thanks for your help today." Dee struggled up from the couch and hugged her sister.

"Sorry to abandon you," Trish said grabbing her jacket, "but I've got to drive Maureen home and then go buy groceries."

"That's it, leave us here with the ghost," Dee said.

"I'm still here you know," a voice echoed from the recliner.

"Both of the ghosts," Sam said.

Maureen shivered. "Right. Whatever. See you tomorrow. I'll bring the candles."

Chapter 11

"I can finish painting the kitchen this afternoon." Sam stood in the living room facing Dee, ignoring the ghosts who were silent for the time being. "I might even be able to get started in the bedroom. But if you want to leave, that's okay too."

Dee reached around his waist and pulled him into a hug pressing her cheek against his shoulder. "I think we should keep working. If you carry the boxes from the kitchen out to your truck, I'll go tackle the master. I can't wait to see how it's going to look with the new color on the walls."

"Don't wear yourself out. If you need a nap, you can always stretch out on the bed."

"I'll be fine," Dee called over her shoulder as she padded off toward the master suite.

She entered the bedroom and took a deep breath. There was no road noise at the back of the house, and Dee relished the quiet. "Hello?" she said into the silence, unaware of Birdie who sat motionless on an armchair near the window.

"I love this view," Dee said. She perched on the rocking chair opposite the armchair and gazed out at the trees. Birdie turned her face away. Dee heaved a big sigh. "But – sooner begun is sooner done."

She picked up the box with the navy leather pumps. "Oh, these *are* nice! I can see why Maureen wanted to try them." With the pregnancy Dee's feet were a bit wider than their usual size. She slipped out of one sneaker and into the leather heel. It fit perfectly.

"Ah-hah! You're not going anywhere," she said, and set the shoes aside in a 'keeping pile' separate from the donations box.

She pulled slacks, dresses, and blouses out of the closet, looking them over and folding them before placing them in the box. "Birdie Ebersole, you took good care of your clothes," she said. "These are going to be a godsend for someone who really needs them."

Birdie glanced her way, then turned toward the window again.

Dee paused at a plum-colored single-breasted jacket with a slim pencil skirt in a soft wool blend with a silky lining. She slipped the jacket off the hanger and tried it on. "Perfect! I'm not going to even try to get into the skirt right now, but in a few months ..."

The last remaining item was inside a long white garment bag. It was tucked so far back in the shadows of the closet that Dee didn't see it until everything else had been removed. She lay the garment bag on the bed and unzipped it. Then she gasped in surprise.

Her fingers traced the intricate lace and pearls on the pristine white bodice and sleeves of an elegant wedding gown. Grasping the padded hanger, she slowly withdrew the heavy gown to reveal a long, full skirt, complete with a sweeping train decorated with more lace appliqués. Its beauty was undiminished by age. It seemed to transcend time.

Dee faced the mirror and held the dress up against her shoulders, pulling the skirt out with one hand. "This is *gorgeous!*" she whispered, feeling an intimate connection to the woman who had worn it years ago.

She lay it on the bed and rummaged in the garment bag again, pulling out a pearl and lace headpiece attached to yards and yards of tulle. She placed it on her head, drawing the netting around her shoulders, and checked the mirror again, smiling as she hummed the wedding march from Wagner's *Lohengrin*.

Beside her, tears rolled down Birdie's cheeks.

Dee stopped humming, and her expression turned sad. She packed the headpiece and the gown carefully into the garment bag and replaced it in the closet.

"How's it going, Sammy?" she asked, rounding the corner into the kitchen. "Oh, wow! Are you finished?"

Sam washed his brush and paint roller in the kitchen sink, careful not to splatter the counter. "Yep. What do you think?"

Dee turned to take in the whole kitchen. "I *love* it! The color works perfectly with the cabinets. It's even better than I expected!" She put her arms around him as he stood at the sink, and leaned her head against his back. "I found your mother's wedding dress."

"Did you? I didn't know she still had it."

"It was packed in a garment bag at the back of her closet. It's gorgeous."

"I thought you didn't like stuff like that. You're a 21st century woman, and don't need all that frippery, or whatever you told me. You don't even want a wedding."

"Well," Dee said, irritated at being reminded, "this is your mom's frippery, and it's pretty. There must be wedding pictures around the house somewhere. I would love to spend an evening going through old pictures."

"Okay," Sam said unenthusiastically.

"Sorry, Sam. I didn't think. Maybe that wouldn't be fun for you right now."

He shrugged his shoulders. "Last time I looked at old pictures it was to find photos of my folks to send to the funeral home. I was just reminded, that's all. But I know exactly where they all are. Wedding pictures, graduation pictures, holiday photos. They're in the closet in the office. In fact, a big wedding album is sitting right on top."

"Do you mind if I check them out sometime?"

"Not at all. Are you ready for me to start painting in the bedroom? I can at least get a little cutting-in done before supper time."

"Do it! I can't wait."

Chapter 12

Sunday evening Dee answered a knock at the door to let her sister in, and was met with a surprise. "Caitlyn! I didn't know you were joining us tonight!"

Caitlyn, Maureen's eight-year-old, sauntered into the living room. "Hi Aunt DeeDee. I want to see the ghost. Is she in here right now?"

"Oh, honey, I don't know. I've never seen her myself. What did you do with Chad?" Dee asked Maureen.

"He's home with his daddy. I forgot that Ryan was having a couple of guys over to watch football tonight. He said he'd keep Chad, but Caitlyn wanted to help with the séance."

"I guess everyone's going to know about the ghosts before long. I wonder if that will make this house the most popular one on the street next Halloween, or keep people away."

"Hopefully the ghosts will just be a distant memory next year. Now, where should I put these candles?" A basketful of jar candles rested on Maureen's hip. Dee glanced at the labels. The wild assortment of scents was guaranteed to drive the people away, if not the ghosts.

"I'm thinking the dining room. We can all sit around the table."

"In the movies the ghost can move the table up and down," Caitlyn explained helpfully.

"We really want this ghost to just go away, Caitlyn, so don't try to make friends with it."

Caitlyn wandered into the living room looking around. Birdie watched in silence as Caitlyn ran her hand along the arm of Martin's recliner. Glancing up suddenly, the child backed away and sat on the couch, staring around her with wide-eyes.

Birdie looked more closely at the child, and her expression softened. She would like to have had a little girl like that, with auburn braids and shoes that glittered with sparkly sequins.

"Knock-knock," Trish said, pushing on the front door. "You're heating the outside, as Mom used to say. This is a pretty safe neighborhood, but you still shouldn't leave your door wide open. By the way, your doorbell doesn't work. Maybe Sam can fix it."

Dee rolled her eyes at the sight of her sister carrying even more candles, in even more scents. "You know, the chandelier in the dining room *is* operational, and from what I've been able to figure out the ghosts aren't afraid of the light."

"In the movie *Ghost in the Twilight*, the ghost busted all the lightbulbs," Caitlyn explained helpfully.

"That's enough, Caitlyn," Maureen said. "Look, Dee-Dee, who's driving this train? It's my séance, done my way." She bustled around arranging candles and shutting the blinds in the front window.

"Yes, Ma'am!" Dee saluted. "Boy, first-borns really are bossy. Are you that bossy, Caitlyn?"

"Yes," the child said.

"Tell 'em, girlfriend." Maureen lit candles with a long lighter.

"Did Sam finish all the painting he was going to do?" Trish asked.

"Yes! He's just putting away his painting gear in the garage. Go look in the bedroom, and show Caitlyn, but don't touch the walls. I love, love, love the gray in there. I've already ordered a new comforter and pillow shams for the bed."

Trish and Caitlyn walked toward the master suite. Birdie followed, watching the sequins glitter on the child's shoes.

Caitlyn headed straight for the upholstered armchair, and bounced on the cushion.

"Oh, this is a nice color," Trish said admiring the freshly-painted walls.

Caitlyn hummed a tune from her favorite cartoon series, gazing through the window at the yard. Dusk had fallen, but a fringe of orange clouds unfurled across the sky.

Birdie hovered nearby. "I like your shoes," she said, and Caitlyn swung her feet up and down. "What is that song? Is it from a movie? Or from a cartoon you like?" She perched on the rocking chair and watched the child, a forlorn expression filling her eyes.

Caitlyn stopped humming.

"What do you think, Caitlyn?" Trish asked, still looking around the room.

"It feels a little sad," the girl said.

"Sad? You're silly. I think it's terrific! Come on. Your mom wants to start the séance."

"Okay, let's get this show on the road," Maureen called clapping her hands. "All my ghostbusters, assemble in the dining room."

Sam came in from the garage and greeted everyone as the group took seats around the table. "Isn't this nice?" Dee said. "If we put the leaf in, we could probably fit the whole family."

"Great. You just volunteered to cook Thanksgiving dinner next year," Trish informed her.

"If I don't have to cook I'll be here, ghost or no ghost," Maureen said.

"I'll have an infant by then," Dee said, a smile lighting her face.

"I'll babysit while you're wrangling the turkey," Trish offered.

"Can we have lots of whipped cream for the pies?" Caitlyn asked. "Mom never lets me have whipped cream."

"Can we have *quiet* so we can start this séance?" Maureen snapped.

Everyone grew silent, exchanging nervous glances or staring at the flickering candles. "Please join hands, and concentrate on the spirits of Birdie and Martin." Obediently they reached for each other's hands.

Sam sat facing the living room. A movement near Martin's recliner caught his attention and he saw his mother materialize, leaning against the chair and surveying the gathering.

"Thank God I can't smell anything," Birdie said. "It looks like every kind of candle known to man is burning in there. I just hope you don't burn the house down!"

"Are the ghosts here yet?" Dee whispered. "I don't want to burn the house down having this séance. That would kind of defeat the purpose." Sam shifted his gaze to Dee, and she giggled.

"Shhh!" Maureen shushed Dee sharply. "They're here. I can feel it."

"Ask them the questions I wrote for you," Sam said.

Maureen gave him a dirty look, and then closed her eyes. "Spirits of the Ebersoles." Her voice took on a low, melodious tone, like she was imitating a Hollywood medium.

"What's up with the voice?" Dee whispered.

"It's like the lady who did the séance in *Ghost in the Twilight*," Caitlyn explained. "Right before her head flopped backwards and her eyes rolled up."

"Shhh!" Maureen shushed everyone, and began again. "Spirits of the Ebersoles, why are you here in the house?"

"Because it's a little too cold for a picnic outside," Birdie answered in a similar tone, and followed it up with a long "Ooooooooo."

Dee shivered, tightening her grip on her neighbors' hands.

Maureen tried again. "Restless spirits, why do you cling to this place? What unfinished business binds you here?"

"Restless spirits!" Birdie clicked her tongue. "Did you come up with that question Samuel, or is Maureen just being creative? Restless. It would be more restful here if these people didn't keep barging into my house!"

Maureen whispered to Sam. "I hear something, but I can't make it out."

"That's okay. She's not saying anything helpful."

Maureen addressed the spirits again. "What can we do to help you pass through the veil? Do you seek release from your loved ones?"

"I don't know about release, but I think my *loved ones* could choose who they associate with a little more carefully." Birdie looked at the adults gathered around the table. "I think my *loved ones* have got themselves into a situation they never intended and are a little too soft-hearted to get themselves out." Now she stared right at Sam. "I don't want to see my *loved ones* doing something they'll regret, *in my house*." She crossed to the dining room, and hovered behind Dee's chair. The temperature in the room seemed to drop a few degrees.

Dee cringed. "I'm getting the distinct feeling the ghosts don't like me."

"I'm cold," Caitlyn said hunching her little shoulders.

"Hush! I'm hearing some words here and there: *loved ones* and *my house*. But I can't understand what she's saying," Maureen said.

"Let me say this loud and clear, then," Birdie shouted, her fists clenched. "*I don't like you people, and I want you all to get the hell out!*" She circled the table with a ghostly moan, flapping her arms, setting the candle flames dancing and the window blinds rattling. "*Get out of my house!*" she screamed again.

Maureen squeezed her eyes shut and shrank down in her chair.

Caitlyn covered her ears. "Mom, what's happening? It feels like someone's yelling."

Trish was the only one who showed any presence of mind. "This has gone far enough. It's just making everyone upset." She rose, letting go of Dee's hand, and switched on the light over the table. The moaning stopped and Birdie's ghost disappeared. Trish started blowing out candles.

Dee sobbed quietly in her seat. Sam scraped back his chair and crouched beside her, putting his arms around her. "It's okay. It's going to be okay," he said over and over, patting her gently. The others pushed away from the table.

Maureen's hands shook as she gathered up candles into her basket. "I knew this was a bad idea," she muttered, casting sorrowful glances at her weeping sister.

Dee pushed Sam away and stood up. "I need to get some air. Trish, take me back to your place." She turned and faced Sam. "Maybe this house isn't right for us after all. I need some time to think. I'll call you."

Trish put an arm around Dee and walked her out the front door.

"Give her a little time," Maureen told Sam. "Meanwhile, I'll think what else we can try. Dee really loved this

house. There's got to be some way to deal with this – problem. Come on Caitlyn." She closed the front door behind
her, leaving Sam alone with the ghosts.

Chapter 13

"What the hell is wrong with you, Ma?" Sam shouted into the empty living room. He stood with hands on hips, scanning the space. "Quit playing games, and come out where I can see you."

Birdie appeared, leaning against the fireplace with her arms folded.

"What is the problem, Ma? First you try to convince me what a wonderful house this is. When I seriously consider moving in you try to drive me out."

"I'm trying to do you a favor," Birdie said. "You have no idea what you're getting yourself into."

"Speak in plain English. Do you mean what I'm getting into becoming a homeowner, or becoming a parent?"

Birdie gave him a dark look and muttered something Sam didn't catch. Martin's voice sounded from the recliner. "That wasn't nice, Birdie."

"What?" Sam asked. "What did she say, Dad?"

Birdie unfolded her arms. "I said, I didn't want you bringing that woman and her little bastard into my house."

Sam reeled as if he had been slapped. Then he straightened, balling his fists. He leaned toward his mother and spoke in a dangerously low voice. "That woman has a name. Her name is Deidre." He raised his voice. "And that is *my* child you're calling a bastard. As far as I'm concerned, they are not negotiable, but this house sure is."

"You're sure it's your child, huh?" Birdie asked.

"Yes, I'm sure. Ma, I've known Dee for years. I've loved Dee since we were kids."

Now it was Birdie's turn to be shocked. "What the hell are you talking about? That kid was in elementary school when her family moved away."

"Dee was fourteen, for your information."

"Oh, my God!" Birdie covered her mouth with her hand and stared at her son. "What did you do to that kid? My own son! Where did I go wrong?"

"We didn't *do* anything, Ma. I said I loved her. I *liked* her. It's not like we ... We never *did* anything Ma. I think maybe we held hands. Maybe I kissed her a couple of times. And then her family moved, and I never saw her again until this summer." His eyes had a faraway look. "But when she came back it was like a piece of me that had been missing was back in place."

He refocused on Birdie. "I love her, Ma. And she loves me, and she's having my child. So you're going to have to deal with it." He lifted his head higher. "Or we'll go some-where where you *won't* have to deal with it. Now which do you want?"

"But you're so young, Samuel, and this is a big step." His mother's tone was pleading.

"I'm twenty-five, Ma. That's not that young. I have a college degree, and a job. The next thing is to find some-one. How long do you want me to wait to get on with my life?"

"That job of yours is nothing to brag about. And in my day the next thing was to *get married,*" she hissed. "You say you love this girl so much and want to do right by her but you're just going to shack up?"

"Oh, get over it Ma! That's bullshit and you know it. I know what the times were like when you were young, with free love and feminism and all that."

Sam turned away, running a hand over the back of his neck in frustration.

"Samuel, are you sure she feels the same as you do? Are you sure she's not just using you?" Birdie's hands were back on her hips. "Look at me. Why don't you just ask her to get married?"

"I *have* asked her, but obviously I can't force her." Birdie smirked. Sam took a step toward her, pointing his finger at her. "It's probably *your* fault, Ma. You know, she idolized you."

"Idolized me? Pfft! I barely even knew the kid. I wouldn't have noticed her except she was up and down the street all the time."

"Yeah, well she sure noticed you." His tone softened. "She admired you. You dressed up in nice clothes and went to work in an office every day. That was something different for Dee. You're the reason she stayed in college. She wanted to have a career, just like you."

"You're kidding me!" Birdie gazed at nothing, a look of wonder on her face.

"Dee has dreams and goals and she's willing to work for them. And frankly, marriage and motherhood were not tops on her list, at least not this soon. She never planned to – to start a family this young. She had this contraceptive patch thing, and I guess it failed. I guess we're the one in a hundred that it doesn't work for. And being pregnant, for her, means having the baby. No discussion. I love her, she loves me, so here we are."

Sam's cell phone rang. He turned away to answer, and Birdie listened to his side of the conversation. "Dee. How are you? No, it's all right. I understand. I'll come get you. Okay. I love you too."

He looked around to find Birdie perched on the arm of the couch, one leg crossed over the other, her hands folded on her knee. "Like I said, Ma. Dee is not negotiable. But the rest of this?" He waved a hand indicating the house. "I really couldn't care less. If you want me to move back here you're going to have to – to keep quiet and stay invisible."

He turned and left the house, slamming the door behind him with a bang.

Chapter 14

Birdie floated blindly through the house replaying the events of the evening in her mind. She had frightened those people at the séance – really frightened them. If she wanted, she could make sure no one ever took up residence in the house.

She tried out her doleful moan again, and whirled through the rooms, rattling the window blinds. She was surprised that she was able to make things move. Maybe it was when she really concentrated. Or was really angry.

She smiled, remembering how she had been able to push Maureen in the bedroom. Boy, she had been mad at Maureen. Who did she think she was, going through her things?

Then Birdie thought of the child Caitlyn, and her smile faded. She wondered if they ever called her Cait, or Caitie. A child like that might try out any number of nicknames over the course of her girlhood.

Birdie thought about the catchy little tune Caitlyn had hummed. She imagined herself watching cartoons, or playing board games, or going out for ice cream with a child that age. A heavy sigh escaped her lips.

"Martin."

"I'm here, Birdie."

That was one of the things she loved about Martin. She never had to worry about where he was, or who he might be running around with. He was always right there. Steady. Patient, while she was out working, or volunteering on some committee or other.

"Did I ever tell you I loved being a mom?"

"Maybe. I can't remember."

"I mean *really* loved it," she said. "More than work, more than all that other stuff. I wish I'd had more kids. I think sometimes I gave Samuel the impression that he wasn't enough. It wasn't that, it was just that I wanted … more. More kids."

"You never told me that," Martin said.

"I know. It was my fault. I guess it was the times, Martin. We were all supposed to be bringing home the bacon and frying it up in the pan, having some big career. Which, don't get me wrong, I enjoyed what I did. I liked being an executive secretary. But I feel like I missed something.

"I don't know why I waited so long to have Samuel. Forty years old. I was always the oldest mom in the momgroups, not that it really bothered me. I loved seeing the kids and the moms. I loved the whole thing. I just wish I had been more present for it. For Motherhood. They tell you that you can have it all, but it's really not true. At least, I couldn't do it."

"You did okay, Birdie," Martin reassured her.

Birdie shook her head. Then she chuckled. "Do you remember the time I took up smoking cigarettes? God, I'm glad that didn't take."

There was a rumbly laugh from the recliner. "I do, vaguely. I don't remember why you did it, though."

"It was the marketing! I wanted to be that feisty gal with the shiner who used to say 'I'd rather fight than switch.' I wanted to be strong, independent, in control! I wanted to be those skinny broads in the Virginia Slims commercials. You remember. 'You've come a long way, baby.'" Birdie laughed bitterly. "I don't know how you put up with me. Hell yes, I came a long way. Only thing was, I was going in the wrong direction. The farther I went, the farther away I got from what *I* really wanted. How does that happen, Martin? We say we're in the groove, but what we mean is we're in a rut. We've gone so far, and can't get out. I wanted to be in control. Maybe I was, for a while. But look where I am now."

"You're home. It's nice to be home," Martin said.

"But it always felt more like home when Samuel was here. Now I've chased him away. Why can't he understand that I just want what's best for him?"

"How do you know what's best for him, Birdie?" Martin asked. "You just said you didn't even know what was best for you. Maybe working at the food bank and building a life with this girl from down the street is what's best for Sammy."

Birdie bobbed on an invisible current, her mouth slightly open, as her husband's words sank in. Unlike Birdie, who had been blown around by the winds of Madison Avenue and the advertising industry, maybe Samuel knew instinctively what would make him happy, and didn't have to chase success, or compare himself to anyone else, or measure up.

She drifted over to Martin's recliner to sit on the arm of the chair, and put her hand on the back of his neck. She used to like weaving her fingers through the short hair at the nape of his neck. He had dropped off to sleep again, and was making a faint snuffling sound as his chest rose and fell.

"Sammy," she said. "That's what *we* used to call him. That's what *she* called him."

Martin stirred, and the snoring stopped. "She who?"

"Deirdre." She breathed another deep sigh. "I guess if we want Samuel to move back home, we'll have to convince Deidre."

Chapter 15

This wasn't the way Sam had intended to start the week.

He'd checked the postal service app on his phone before he left work, irritated to see how much mail was still being delivered to his parents' old house. He sighed, and turned his pickup truck toward Fairlawn Street.

He was tired of running to the place so often, but today he had to retrieve the mail. The app had informed him the bill for the homeowner's insurance had been delivered. God forbid anything should happen to the house between now and whenever he sold the place, moved in, or whatever was going to happen. He didn't want the insurance to lapse the day before lightning struck or a tree fell on the roof.

He had cancelled the magazine subscriptions and changed a few addresses, but what was the point of rerouting all his parents' mail to his apartment if he wasn't going to be staying there much longer either?

He slowed for a group of kids playing kickball. He remembered playing games like that, growing up in the neighborhood. He was glad to see that kids still did that sort of thing. As the weather got colder and the snow started it would be street hockey. He regretted now that he'd thrown away the old hockey stick he'd discovered at the back of his closet. But he hadn't played in over ten years. Was it just ten, or even longer?

The kids cleared out of the street and Sam pulled into the drive. He noticed a package on the porch, so after unlocking the door he turned on the porch lights and carried the package inside. Then he fetched the mail and dropped the letters on the dining room table.

There was no sign of his parents anywhere, but he had an uneasy feeling that he was missing something. Everything was *too* quiet, like the house was holding its breath. He walked into the living room to glance at his father's recliner and listen a moment longer.

Shaking his head, he returned to the dining table to open the mail. He was about to write out a check when a loud rap at the front door made him jump.

What he saw through the sidelights made his eyes pop. He regained his composure and opened the door to an attractive woman who greeted him with a gleaming smile.

Martin had been right. Sam's ex-girlfriend Amber was a real looker, and the years since they'd parted company hadn't hurt her a bit. The woman was tall and slim, with curves where it mattered. Her long hair framed her face in loose waves, and her make-up was TV-interview ready.

She wore tight jeans and a pink cashmere sweater under her creamy wool jacket. The whole outfit had the casual look that cost a lot of money to achieve.

"Well if it isn't Sam Ebersole!" she said, adjusting the expensive bag on her shoulder and striking a pose.

"Amber! What a surprise." Reluctantly he stepped aside and invited her in with a wave of his hand. "Uh, what brings you here?"

"I saw that the house was listed, and called your realtor for a showing. By the way, I'm so sorry about the loss of your parents. I heard the news about the bridge collapsing and everything. That video – how awful!" She grimaced, turning down her lipstick-covered lips in a frown that reminded him of a clown face. All she needed was a few painted-on tears.

"Yes, it was awful," Sam muttered in agreement. His heart ached whenever someone commented on the tragedy. He wished they would just stop. It did nothing to comfort him, and made *them* seem more like voyeurs than people who actually cared. Their fascination felt ghoulish.

Amber walked farther into the entryway, looking around. "You know, I'm working in town now. I saw the listing on this house, and wanted to take a look. All on one floor, established lawn, enough yard to putter around in." She waited for Sam to say something, but when he remained mute she went on. "I thought the realtor was here. Bob – whatever his name is. I guess I should have recognized your old truck outside."

Sam ground his teeth. His truck wasn't that old. Why, ten years was nothing on a pick-up truck! Everyone knew trucks kept their value much better than cars. He peeked past Amber through the sidelight to see what she was driving. A sleek black sedan with gold trim was parked at the curb. The kids playing kickball were nowhere in sight.

Amber's phone dinged. She plunged a manicured hand deep into her designer bag and glanced at the text. "Oh, Bob's on his way. Says he was held up but he'll be here shortly." She leaned in and said in a conspiratorial whisper, "He tells me your parents are *still here*."

Sam could feel the blood drain from his face. He walked stiff-legged into the living room. "Why don't we sit down while we wait for Bob."

She followed him, and started to sit in the recliner.

Sam lunged for her arm. "You can't sit there!" he said, dragging her to her feet with such force that she crashed into him.

They stood momentarily in an awkward embrace. Then Sam loosened his grip on her arm and Amber pushed him away with her free hand on his chest. "Why can't I sit there?" she asked, studying the recliner with wide eyes.

"It's ... It's broken. Here. Sit on the couch. It's really comfortable."

"All righty then." She looked warily at him, rubbing her arm, and perched on the edge of the couch ready to leap up and run to the door at the next outburst.

She looked over at the mantel and her expression softened. She pointed at the funerary urns. "Like Bob said. Your parents *are* still here."

"Yes! My parents. *Those* are my parents. Inside the urns." Sam rubbed the back of his neck, feeling a little shaky.

"Not that it's really my business, Sam, but don't you think the house would show better without people's ashes in the living room?" She crossed her long legs and quirked a shapely eyebrow at him.

Sam swallowed hard. "Bob was fine with it, so..." He desperately wanted to change the subject. "You said you're working in town now. How's that going for you?"

"Yes." Her gleaming smile returned. "I'm working for Statewide Insurance Company. I landed a junior executive position, and they've already made me permanent. Which means I'll be staying with the company and building my career there." She looked puzzled for a moment. "Remind me where you're working again?"

Sam mumbled something that Amber didn't catch. She cocked her head.

"I said, Gracious Plenty Food Bank."

"Oh! The food bank!" Amber didn't exactly sneer, but she did smirk. "You should apply at Statewide. They're always looking for people who understand business, and with your degree I'm sure you could land one of the trainee slots."

Sam remained silent. One thing Amber and his mother had agreed on was that his business degree was wasted at a non-profit. He knew he could make more money elsewhere, but that was not the point.

Food insecurity was not just a personal problem, it was a community problem. More than half the people the food bank served made too much money to qualify for food stamps. That meant they were working. They were working hard, but still struggling, having to make trade-offs about which bills to pay and which to hold off on. It impacted their stress levels and their health. It made it harder for them to show up and be productive at work, and harder for their kids to participate in school and actually learn.

Sam sighed. He wasn't interested in defending his choice of employment with someone who had left him for a frat boy, born with a silver spoon up his ... whatever. Sam had thought he was over the anger and hurt he felt at Amber's betrayal, but apparently not. The silence stretched between them, growing awkward.

Amber took a compact out of her purse and looked at herself in the mirror, then snapped it closed with a click. "Anyway, from the pictures online this looks like a great little house. So cozy, with vintage charm."

Sam wondered if she moonlighted writing advertising copy for a real estate listing service. The adjectives she used were synonyms for "cramped" and "old." He couldn't understand why she was even interested.

He still wasn't sure he wanted the house for himself, but he was starting to think he didn't want to sell it to Amber. "Actually, I'm thinking of taking the house off the market. My fiancée and I have been discussing moving in."

"Your fiancée! Well, congratulations on your upcoming nuptials. Who's the lucky girl?" Amber purred.

"Her name is Dee Malloy. Deirdre."

"Deirdre." Amber's forehead creased. "Wasn't that the name of the girl you told me about? The one who moved away?"

Sam cursed silently, and nodded. He should never have told Amber about Dee. "She has family in town, working at City Hospital. She's living with her sister."

Amber looked Sam up and down. "Well, well. The first love is the best love, or whatever it is they say. When's the wedding?"

"Er ... We haven't set the date yet."

At last there was a knock on the door, and Sam rose to open it. The realtor greeted Sam, and then made a beeline for Amber, giving her a weak handshake. Bob wasted no time extolling the house's features, pointing out the woodburning fireplace which had just been inspected. Sam watched in fascination as the man's Adam's apple bobbed up and down.

He returned to his paperwork at the dining table while the two moved on through the house. He could hear Bob droning on about its salient features, switching on every light as he went.

Sam finished with the bill-paying chores, and decided to open the package that had been left on the porch. Inside he found the bedding Dee ordered. It was silvery-gray and shades of ocean blue in a wavy pattern.

Hastily he closed the box as Amber and Bob returned from the master suite. He did not want to discuss bedding with his ex-girlfriend. No doubt she had opinions about that, but he didn't care to hear them. There's something very personal about a bed, Sam thought. If he ever moved in here he might need to buy a new one.

"The house is exactly what I'm looking for," she crowed. "It has lots of income potential, and the rental market is hot right now."

Sam's mouth dropped open. "Income potential! You want to turn this house into a rental?"

"You didn't think I wanted it for myself, did you?" Amber's amused expression made the color rise in Sam's face. She didn't seem to notice. "I know from the listing what the asking price is. I'd like to make an offer."

Sam expected her to counter the asking price with something several thousand dollars lower. After all, he figured she must also know how long the house had been on the market.

She surprised him by making a preemptive bid, more than the realtor had estimated would be top dollar.

Sam's eyebrows rose. "That's a very generous offer." Behind Amber the realtor nodded up and down, pantomiming, "Say yes!"

Chapter 16

Sam's eyes shifted uneasily from Bob to Amber. It was a lot of money, enough to tip the balance on his decision concerning the house. He was still angry with his mom, and not at all sure if Dee would cross the threshold ever again. But something made him hesitate.

"If you don't mind, I'd like a couple of days to consider, and to discuss it with my fiancée. Can I let you know by Friday?"

Amber looked surprised he didn't jump at her offer. "I'm not used to people turning me down," she said, looking along her shapely nose at him. "But since you're an old friend, I'll wait until Friday." She turned to the realtor. "Meanwhile Bob can show me the *other* houses we had lined up." She glanced sideways at Sam, hoping that would nudge him in the direction of accepting.

Instead, Sam nudged Amber and the realtor toward the door. "It was good to see you again, Amber. I'll be sure to call you by Friday with my decision. Thanks for stopping by."

Sam watched through the sidelight until their cars pulled away from the curb. Then he sat at the dining room table and palmed his eyes thinking about the exchange with Amber.

It was a generous bid on the house, he had to admit. Her offer exceeded the recent comps in the neighborhood by at least a few thousand. If she was trying to convince him to sell, she had done her homework.

With that offer he could make a down payment on something newer. There were some swanky new townhouses and starter homes being built closer to work and to downtown. He could leave behind his worries about whether he could ever be happy in the house on Fairlawn Street. And leave behind the ghosts.

He was not entirely sure about that last thought. Just because he hadn't encountered the two spirits anywhere besides the house didn't mean he wouldn't. Did it? Would they haunt him wherever he went?

The phone rang and Sam jumped. He fumbled for it on the table, knocked it onto the floor, retrieved it, and swiped the screen before he even looked to see who was calling.

"Hi. What did you think of that offer?" It was Bob. Sam was surprised to hear something like glee in the man's voice, since everyone agreed he had the personality of a dead fish.

"Hi, Bob. Yeah, it was quite a bit higher than the comps, wasn't it," Sam said, stating the obvious.

"Sure was. Looks like you've got yourself a buyer." Sam could almost see Bob's smug smile over the phone. "I can call the lawyer tomorrow to get the paperwork started."

"Hold on, Bob. Like I said, I'd like a day or two to think it over. I can give you a call no later than Friday." Sam swallowed.

"Sam, you'd be a fool to turn down this offer. Especially considering how long your house has been on the market."

There was a lengthy pause. "Sam?"

"I said I'd think about it, Bob. Look, it's late. I promise I'll call you by the end of the week. Have a good night." Sam ended the call before Bob could insult him again. *I'm paying the guy*, Sam thought, *and he's calling me a fool?*

Actually he hadn't paid Bob anything, Sam realized, which was why the realtor was pushing for the sale. Still, it was the principal. It was Sam's decision whether to sell, and to whom. He didn't need Bob twisting his arm.

The phone rang again and he looked at it with irritation. His expression changed when he saw who the caller was. "Hi, Dee. What's up?" He straightened the papers on the dining table.

"I made us some supper. Did you get stuck at work, or ...?"

"No, I ran by the house on Fairlawn to take care of a couple of bills. The insurance on the house, and what-not.

Then Bob was here to show someone the house. It was someone I knew in college, so that took a little time."

"It wasn't that Amber, was it? The one whose picture you showed me?"

Damn, Sam thought. When would he learn to keep his mouth shut? He realized his reply was taking too long. "Yeah, actually. It was," he said.

"Does she still look like a super-model?" Dee asked.

Sam thought he heard jealousy in her voice. "I didn't notice."

Dee had been fretting lately about all the changes to her body, and not feeling attractive. Sam had reassured her as best he could. Really there was no comparison between the two women. He loved the new softness of Dee's body, how beautiful her hair was, the fullness of her breasts. He closed his eyes, picturing her, and took a deep breath remembering her scent.

"Hmph. Didn't notice, huh?" Dee commented. "What's she doing these days? I didn't know she was even anywhere around here."

"Working at Statewide Insurance, she said."

"That sweatshop? I know some people in the IT department there. They hate it." She paused. "Well, what did she think of the house?"

Sam let out a breath. "Oh, you know. She'd never want to live in this neighborhood." At least that part was true.

"She mentioned hearing that my parents died, and seeing the accident video and everything. I think it was partly just morbid curiosity. She seemed fixated on the urns on the mantle. I don't have time for gawkers. Bob can handle her."

"Well, come home soon so we can eat together, okay? I'm starving."

"Okay. Love you." He touched the screen to end the call, and leaned back in the chair.

What would he do if he sold the house? He thought again about the upscale new homes he'd seen going up in town. They were really nice. Probably they were the reason this house wasn't selling.

He sighed. He just wasn't the fashionable, upscale type.

Not like Amber. She probably lived in one of those posh places. It was pretty ridiculous that he had thought she might be interested in moving to Fairlawn Street. He couldn't see her grilling in the back yard with any of the neighbors.

But that offer she'd made... Why was she so willing to pay top dollar for 'vintage' and 'cozy'? Was she doing Sam a favor? Poor Sam, who was throwing his life away on some job that couldn't pay him what his mother thought he was worth? He felt judged and insulted again.

What would become of the neighborhood if it started having a bunch of rental properties and absentee landlords? What would the neighbors think? What would his mother think?

Call him vindictive, but if selling Amber this house would make her happy – the woman who had cheated on him and left him with a broken heart – or a bruised heart, anyway – then he was inclined to do the exact opposite.

He stacked up the mail he had come to retrieve and started switching off lights. Dee was waiting for him at the apartment.

Now *there* was a place devoid of personality and charm. Not to mention he was tired of looking out his living room window at a parking lot. Maybe vintage and cozy were just what he needed. Something that felt familiar and comfortable, after his current, generic apartment.

He took a second look at the new bedding Dee had ordered. She must have known blue was his favorite color. The ripples in the design reminded him of water and sunshine playing on the bottom of a swimming pool. He carried the large comforter to the bedroom, spreading it out on the bed.

He tweaked it a few times to straighten it out, then returned to the dining room for the shams. He stuffed his parents' old pillows inside, propped them at the head of the bed, and stood back to take in the effect. His eyes swept from the newly painted walls to the sitting area near the window and back to the bed.

Then he flopped down on it. He closed his eyes and imagined he was floating. He hadn't been swimming at the rec center in a week, and had the urge to swim now. In the pool the water muffled the sound of everything, and all he had to think about was the rhythm of his arms, his legs, his breath. He wanted to just swim and swim, lap after lap, away from everything.

Away from everything, except that in his mind's eye Dee was waiting for him at the edge of the pool. Waiting with a baby in her arms.

Chapter 17

Amber tapped her foot, waiting on the front porch for Bob to come unlock the house on Fairlawn Street. Her lunch hour would be over if he didn't hurry, and the home remodeler waiting with her didn't have all day either.

"Sorry to keep you waiting," Bob said with an ingratiating smile. He fiddled with the lock box. Seconds later he swung open the front door and the three stepped inside.

Birdie hovered near the ceiling, a dim misty shadow. When she'd first seen Amber the night before, she didn't know what to think. With Dee pregnant it would not be a good thing for Sam's old girlfriend to come back into his life.

When Birdie realized Amber wanted to turn the house into a rental, she had nearly gone through the roof. And now the woman was back with a remodeler. This was not good.

"Lots of natural light, which you couldn't really see last night," Bob commented, pointing to the windows in the dining room and living room.

"I think the ceilings need repainting." Amber glanced upward, and Birdie shrank into a corner. "And those trees in the back yard are too close to the house. They'll have to come down."

Birdie gasped audibly and covered her mouth, but no one seemed to hear her.

"I'll call the tree service to get an estimate," Bob mumbled, scribbling a note in the small pad of paper he carried.

Amber summoned the remodeler with a crook of her manicured finger. "Tell me what it's going to take to tear down this wall between the living room and the kitchen and put in a nice big island."

Birdie's eyes bulged. She flew between the living room and the kitchen, no longer worried about keeping herself concealed.

It broke her heart to think of the wall of cabinetry being taken down. There would be no room to store things! Besides, she loved her kitchen. Sam and Dee loved the kitchen. A kitchen should be its own place, a sanctuary. She remembered the time spent in the intimacy of her grandmother's kitchen. It wouldn't be the same with the house wide open.

She followed the remodeler as he stretched out his tape measure and sketched a drawing on some paper on the kitchen counter.

Amber strolled off through the house poking her head into closets, cupboards, and drawers, and Birdie sailed after her. Why had she thought the girl was so attractive, Birdie wondered? When her model's smile slipped, her face took on a snooty expression.

They returned to the kitchen. "I'm going to want to gut the two bathrooms, so I'll need an estimate for that. And Bob, didn't you say there's attic access through the garage? I'd like to see if it's possible to put in a couple of dormers and create a bonus room up there."

Birdie was a little intrigued by that idea, until she remembered the girl didn't want the house to live in herself.

The remodeler bent to examine the electrical outlets above the countertop, and Birdie circled around the kitchen, creating a small whirlwind that scattered his papers all over the floor.

Amber covered her head, trying to keep her perfect hair in place while Bob leaped around the kitchen like a grasshopper retrieving the papers.

"What was that all about? Is there a fan in here?" Amber pushed the buttons on the stove vent, which hummed obligingly but failed to create much of a breeze.

"Let's look in the garage," Bob said, ushering Amber through the back door. He pulled down the rickety stairs and climbed up to pull on the light chain dangling through the access door. "There's some flooring up here. You can see the previous owners used it for storage. Looks like they left you a Christmas tree. But there's plenty of room, and a lofty ceiling."

He came down and Amber climbed up to have a look for herself. Birdie had got there ahead of her, and as Amber glanced around, the ghost whirled up a cloud of old dust and bits of pink insulation.

"Ick! All this dust in my eyes! My hair!" She clattered back down the stairs, losing one of her stylish flats in the process. "What is it with the air flow in this place?"

Bob stammered, wide eyed, "Maybe it's the attic vents in the gables." He climbed the stairs for another look. "We'll have the inspector check them out. Of course, if they need any repair it'll be the seller's responsibility."

"It might take longer than I thought to get this place ready to rent," Amber said. "I'm going back in." Bob folded the stairs, closed up the access door and followed her.

The remodeler was taking measurements in the hall bathroom now. Amber looked over his shoulder, then glanced at her watch and heaved a sigh. She walked into the living room, brushing at her hair to remove the dust and bits of fiberglass.

"I can stay here with the remodeler if you need to get back to work," Bob offered, taking a seat on the couch.

"I can wait a bit longer. I really want to see his preliminary estimates." Amber leaned a hand on the arm of Martin's chair and removed one shoe, shaking some pink insulation out of it. She did the same with her other shoe, and sighed once again.

She took a good look at the recliner. "Is this thing okay?" she asked. "The seat cushion looks a little deflated." Rather than sitting on the couch with Bob, she sat on the edge of the chair.

She slid back, trying to get more comfortable, but a second later bounced out of the recliner with a yelp. "It pinched me! There's something in that chair!" She stared down at the cushion.

Bob rushed over, but wouldn't get too close to the recliner.

Amber stared at Bob, and then narrowed her eyes looking accusingly at him. "This place doesn't have some kind of *bug-infestation*, does it? You're supposed to disclose that, you know. Is that why Sam didn't want me sitting here?"

Birdie glided past them and squeezed up the chimney to create another whirlwind. A gray cloud of ash puffed out of the fireplace and into the living room.

Amber shrieked, snatched her designer bag from the entryway and rocketed out the door. Bob dashed after her. "I'll call the chimney sweep this afternoon," he hollered.

"Call anyone you want as long as it's not me! This buyer is no longer interested!" Her car door slammed and Amber took off down Fairlawn Street.

"Do you think she still wants these estimates?" the remodeler asked Bob, clipping his tape measure onto his belt.

The realtor shook his head. "Who knows what she wants. It's the story of my life – women who can't make up their minds. Probably because they don't have any brains in their heads."

Birdie kicked up one last whirlwind, flinging all the business cards and real-estate flyers off the dining room table. Bob gulped, his Adam's apple bobbing as he fled from the house.

Chapter 18

Dee kissed Sam goodbye and left the apartment early Saturday morning to spend the day with Maureen. Minutes later Sam jumped in his truck and pulled off on errands of his own.

He hadn't said anything to her about the offer he'd received for the house on Fairlawn Street. He had made up his mind. He knew what he wanted now, and just hoped Dee wanted the same thing.

But if he was going to convince her to move into the house, he had to be sure his parents weren't going to interfere. And he had to make the place as inviting as possible. He had some ideas, and was ready to put his plans in motion.

His first stop was the hardware store. Dee had mentioned changing out the hardware on the kitchen cabinets and drawers. He had counted them up, and figured since the current hardware was shiny brass he would look for whatever was the opposite.

He settled for brushed nickel, which the salesman assured him was very popular. Sam hoped that going with 'popular' wasn't a mistake. He'd come to terms with the fact that he didn't normally like whatever was popular. He was definitely outside of the mainstream.

He also picked out two new light fixtures, again with the help of the salesman. Then he called Chris Johnson, a client and part-time worker at the food bank. Chris was always up for an odd job if it put a little extra change in his pocket.

"If you have a ladder and a few tools, I can swap out those light fixtures," Chris assured him.

Sam picked up Chris on his way to the house on Fairlawn. The two entered through the garage so Sam could fetch the ladder and tools. While Chris examined the light fixture over the work area, Sam took a quick look around.

The house was still. Not in a holding-its-breath kind of way; but in a peaceful way. Sam closed his eyes, and exhaled as his heart rate slowed down.

"Hey!" Chris said suddenly. Sam returned to the kitchen and looked up to see Chris near the top of the ladder handing down the old fixture. "Grab this and hand me the new one."

Sam rushed to take it from him. He unboxed the new light and carefully handed it up, glad the salesman had suggested he buy a few light bulbs. Next Chris tackled the light over the kitchen table, and soon had it swapped out as well.

The two spent the better part of an hour changing out cabinet knobs and drawer pulls. When they were done, Sam had to admit that between the new additions, the fresh paint on the walls, and all the cleaning Dee and her sisters had done, the kitchen looked great.

"One more job to do," Sam said. "I need to pull up some carpet in one of the bathrooms. I have no idea what's underneath it, so keep your fingers crossed."

They passed through the living room and Chris noticed the urns on the mantel piece. "Holy crap. Are those what I think they are?"

"Um, yes." Sam wished for the umpteenth time that his parents had made their desires known. Beyond them wanting to be cremated, they'd never told him anything.

"What are you going to do with them?" Chris asked. "I mean, while I'm here I could dig a hole in the back yard." Sam's jaw dropped. "Save you some money, man, that's all I'm saying. The whole earth is sacred, you know what I mean?"

Sam closed his mouth and gave Chris's suggestion some thought.

Suddenly the air pressure in the house changed. Sam felt like he couldn't breathe. He looked anxiously around the living room, wondering if his parents had heard and were making their feelings known. He worked his jaw up and down, trying to get his ears to pop.

Chris seemed to feel something too. "This is some strange weather we're having today. It's not supposed to rain, but it sure does feel like it. Makes my knees hurt." He moved to sit in the recliner.

"Don't sit down!" Sam shouted, his heart climbing into his throat.

Chris jumped into the middle of the room, turning to stare at the chair.

"It was my dad's. I don't like anyone else sitting there."

"It's okay, man. I understand," Chris said. He put a hand on Sam's shoulder, and looked him in the eye. "Relax. We're cool. Let's go check out that carpet."

Sam led the way down the short hall, looking nervously around when they got to the bedroom. That still, peaceful feeling was gone, but at least his mother was keeping quiet and staying invisible, just as he'd asked.

He said a hasty prayer as Chris took a utility knife and made the first cut into the bathroom carpet. It came up easily, revealing almost-new tile underneath. Sam and Chris exchanged a high five. Then they ripped up all the old carpet and carried it to the trash can.

They returned to the master bedroom and Sam gathered up the tools. "Can you carry that little rocking chair to the other bedroom? We're going to set it up as a nursery, and I think a rocking chair in there would be nice."

While Chris carried the chair through the house, Sam debated what to do with his dad's recliner. He couldn't stand guard over it all the time, but the idea of people sitting on his dad's lap was more than he wanted to contemplate.

It was hard for him to believe he was worrying about rearranging a ghost's furniture, but there it was. Maybe they could move the recliner into the garage. Dad had enjoyed puttering with his tools out there, and his mom could still find him when she wanted his opinion on something.

His parents drove him batty sometimes, but one thing he'd admired about their relationship was how they were always there for each other, like a couple of gears in a well-oiled machine. It was fitting that they had been in that accident together. As in life, so in death, he thought, or however the saying went.

He breathed a heavy sigh. Chris was waiting for orders with his hands on his hips. "Okay, last thing," Sam said. "These recliners always weigh a ton. You take that side, and I'll take this side." Together they moved it to its new home, next to his dad's old workbench.

Sam paid Chris what he owed him, and they swung by Hardee's for a bite before he dropped Chris off. Then Sam headed back to Fairlawn to make a couple more phone calls. He had one more thing to arrange.

He hoped Dee would be pleased with his efforts – if he ever got her back into the house.

Chapter 19

"What am I going to do, Maureen?" Dee twirled a stir-stick in her latte, scooped up some foamed milk, and licked it off. "I mean, we're running out of time."

"Well, that last one we looked at was plenty big enough, and move-in ready. Even came with a garage! That's like gold around here." Maureen and Dee watched from a table on the periphery while Caitlyn and Chad played video games at Retrocade Coffee. It was the reward Maureen had promised her kids for being patient while the two women dragged them along to check out some apartments.

"I almost had to get nasty with that leasing agent," Dee said. "She was being so pushy, and I'm always suspicious when they say 'last chance' and 'sign now before someone else takes it.' That doesn't change the facts, though. Sam's lease is up on the apartment in another month. If we don't move into his parents' house, we need to do something else really quick. And I'd hate to move into one place, only to have to move again in another year."

Maureen nibbled a bite out of her cookie. "It does seem like your life is moving too fast. Then again, I didn't know you've had a crush on Sam since middle school," Maureen mused. "I guess I missed a lot of your 'formative years.' You were just some little kid riding around the neighborhood on that bike of yours. By the time you got interesting I was having babies and you were headed to college."

"Yeah, our lives haven't meshed very well, considering we share the same parents. I can't believe I never knew about your psychic abilities," Dee countered.

"I stay as far away from ghosts as possible. I couldn't live in that house on Fairlawn, unless someone figured out how to tame the spirits, or evict them, or something. Do you think Sam can get them under control?"

"Who knows. I'm not one hundred percent sure what he wants at the moment. He's still grieving, and meanwhile he's been busy with all that executor-of-the-estate stuff, closing out accounts, worrying about taxes, and on and on. We're both going through some tough times." Dee heaved a great sigh. "I just want the world to stop spinning for a while. It makes me dizzy."

"Here. Have a piece of cookie." Maureen broke off a piece for Dee and then took another nibble. "It's delicious. Although the pleasure is somewhat diminished by the calorie count posted on the bakery display case. And, as a nutritionist, I know what it's doing to my arteries."

"They should have been more specific when they told me I needed to take in more calories while I was expecting. I sure have been taking advantage. Do you bake at home much?"

"Last time I baked cookies I used one of the healthy recipes I share with my clients. The kids each ate one and then asked if we had any Oreos. Cretins. You have to have a certain maturity to appreciate a healthy homemade cookie."

"I've been dreaming about baking lately. I haven't wanted to make a mess in Trish's place. It's always too *clean*. And Sam's gloomy apartment doesn't inspire me. But I've been picturing myself in my new kitchen with a cute vintage apron on."

"Which 'new kitchen' would that be?" Maureen quirked an eyebrow. "You really see yourself in that house on Fairlawn, don't you."

"I do. I feel drawn to that place, like I have a sentimental attachment to it, even though I've never lived there before. But I want Sam to be happy. And I want my family to be able to come visit me there." She breathed a big sigh. "I just need the ghosts to move on."

Chapter 20

"Chapel of the Winds. How can I help you?"

It sounded like an elderly lady on the other end, Sam thought. He hoped his question didn't freak her out. "Uh, yes. This is Sam Ebersole. My parents were married at Chapel of the Winds about thirty-five years ago."

Sam had seen the wedding photos when he'd selected pictures for the funeral slide-show. The chapel featured a quaint-looking, vaguely-churchy, non-denominational building in a park-like setting, along with an outdoor wedding space and reception facilities. His parents had held their small wedding and reception all on-site.

"That's wonderful!" The person on the other end sounded cheery. "Are you looking for a place to hold an anniversary party?"

"Uh. No." The question flustered Sam. He wondered if their anniversary *was* coming up. He dragged his thoughts back to the present. "No. Unfortunately, they both passed away earlier this year."

"Oh. I *am* sorry. My condolences, Mr. Ebersole." She sounded sympathetic now, and waited for Sam to get to the point.

"I'm calling to ask if you have someplace on the grounds near the chapel where their ashes might be scattered." Sam waited for what seemed like a long time, wondering if what he had asked was out in left field. He could hear papers shuffling in the background.

"Your request is quite common, actually. Many people have asked to scatter the ashes of loved ones here, but I'm afraid we don't allow that. As you know Chapel of the Winds is on a hillside overlooking a valley, and it does get breezy out here. Human remains could *blow around* as you might imagine, and get everywhere if you tried to scatter them here, which is not good especially if we're holding an outdoor wedding."

That was a visual Sam knew he wouldn't be able to erase from his mind soon.

"May I ask, are the ashes in some type of urn, or other container?" she asked.

"Yes. They're in urns." Sam held his breath, feeling more hopeful.

"Let me share some of the options for our columbarium."

"You have a columbarium?" Sam asked. "Like, with niches for urns, and such?" He was surprised, but then he only thought of the place in terms of weddings, when he thought of it at all.

"Oh, yes. It's something we added about twenty years ago. Our columbarium is quite large. It's solid granite, forming a walled garden. There's a lovely fountain in the middle, granite benches and so forth. It's a beautiful, peaceful place. You'll find a few pictures on our website, but you really need to see it in person to appreciate how lovely it is."

Sam's mood brightened. After some discussion he purchased a deep niche that could accommodate both urns, and promised to call back to schedule the appointment for the inurnment. He was hoping Dee would go with him, and that he could do it soon.

Maybe even today.

Chapter 21

"It's called Chapel of the Winds," Sam told Dee over the phone.

"Never heard of it," Dee said. "Chapel of the Winds," she repeated for Maureen's benefit, and then put the call on speaker.

"Well, you've seen it. It's where my parents got married, so it's in the wedding photos."

"Oh! And now you're going to scatter their ashes there?" Dee asked uncertainly.

"No, I've paid for a large niche in the columbarium."

"Columbarium." Dee mouthed the word to Maureen, and flashed a thumbs-up.

"I bet people are dying to get in," Maureen whispered.

"I'm getting the urns out of the house on Fairlawn Street. I was hoping you'd go with me." There was a wistful note in Sam's voice.

"Of course I'll go with you. Do I need to dress up, or anything? I've just got these old jeans on." She hoped she wouldn't have to change out of her comfy shoes. She'd been on her feet for way too long, but didn't want to tell

Sam that, or that she and Maureen had been apartment hunting all morning.

"Whatever you have on is fine. I can come pick you up, or Maureen can bring you, whichever works."

Dee looked up 'Chapel of the Winds' on her phone's map, which told her it was twenty minutes away. Her sister nodded. "Maureen says she'll drop me off, but she won't stay. She has to get her kids home."

"That's fine. I'm still at the house on Fairlawn. I'll leave here in about five minutes, and meet you at the chapel.

* * *

"This is sort of a cute place," Dee said as Maureen pulled up the drive.

"Now I remember, I was here for a wedding about ten years ago," Maureen said. "The chapel was pretty, as I recall. I didn't realize you could be buried here too though."

"Full service. I wonder what they'll add next. Maybe a water park?"

"Water park! Water park!" Chad and Caitlyn chanted from the back seat.

"Hush. It's not really funny," Maureen said with a glance at Dee.

Dee's expression suddenly turned sober. "No, it's not. Poor Sammy."

They read the signs pointing to the chapel, the reception hall, and the memorial garden. "There's the office," Dee said. "Just drop me there."

Sam sat waiting for her inside. His face reflected a touching blend of grief and quiet resolve which tugged at Dee's heart. He stood, and Dee wrapped her arms around him.

"This is Barbara," Sam said when they'd stepped apart, introducing the receptionist.

The women shook hands, and Barbara smiled at Dee's round belly. "Let me just get the keys, and we can take the golf cart around to 'the garden.' It's not far from here, and you're welcome to walk or to drive yourself in future, but this way I can show you your niche, and you'll see where everything is."

Dee glanced around the office and spotted the urns with Martin's and Birdie's remains. They looked strangely lonely now that they were no longer on the mantel in the living room. She felt a stab of sorrow that Sam's parents were gone so soon.

Barbara returned, and Sam went to pick up the urns. "Would you like me to carry one?" Dee asked.

Sam took a deep breath. "No," he said, bending his knees slightly and taking one in each arm. "I've got them. This is the last thing I can do for them."

Dee hadn't seen Sam looking this somber since the funeral. She followed him silently out to the waiting golf cart and listened with one ear while Barbara chattered on.

"We had an extended family visiting here recently," Barbara said, "and I gave an elderly gentleman a ride in the golfcart. His little grandson wanted to ride too, and asked his grandpa where they were going. The man said, 'to visit Grandma.' Well, the little boy's eyes got as big as saucers, and he asked his grandpa, 'Is this heaven?' It's not heaven, but it is a beautiful spot. Some people inquire about having their weddings outdoors right here, before they realize what it is."

Barbara was right. It was a pretty place, with sunshine playing on the water splashing gently in the fountain. The flower beds had been cleaned up in preparation for winter, but they could tell the formal gardens would be beautiful come spring. The columbarium formed a low wall around the garden, making it feel secluded from the rest of the grounds. Benches were placed here and there so people could sit when they came 'to visit Grandma.'

"Here's your niche. We'll leave the number on it until the bronze plaque arrives. We tell people it takes two weeks, but they're usually ready sooner." She unlocked the niche and stepped back. "Take as long as you want.

You can call me at the office number and I'll pick you up again with the golfcart." Barbara left them alone.

Sam looked at Dee, the corners of his mouth turned down. "Here, can you hold this?" he asked, handing her Martin's urn. "I guess I'll put Ma in first, and that way Dad can be next to the door." He slid the first urn in, and then placed the second one behind it. Very slowly, he pushed the door closed, and it locked into place.

Dee reached for his hand, and led him to the nearest bench where the two sat down. "This feels really strange," he said, and then swallowed down the lump in his throat.

"Stranger than taking the urns from the funeral home to Fairlawn Street?" Dee asked.

"No, probably not." Sam started to laugh. "I guess a lot of people are comforted to think their parents are in a better place, or whatever. Since mine seem to be still at the old house, I don't guess we can say that." He smiled at Dee, but his expression quickly turned serious.

"I'd like you to take one more look at the house, Dee." The wind ruffled his hair as he gazed deeply into her eyes. "I think we need to give the place one more chance. Ma promised to keep quiet and stay invisible. What do you say."

"I'll go to the house on Fairlawn with you," Dee said. Right now, she thought, I would go with you anywhere.

Chapter 22

By the next day Dee was having second thoughts.

"Sammy, I'm not so sure I can do this. It's like you said. Your parents are still in that house! Last time I was there your mom made it clear she wanted us out. The place is just too crowded." Dee toyed with the crust of her pizza, and then shoved the plate away from her. "Poor Maureen. To think that she's been dealing with ghosts for years!"

Sam looked up at the ceiling. How was it that every time they ate at Mario's they ended up sitting right under a speaker? And why did it have to be playing "The House of the Rising Sun," of all things? It made it hard to have a serious conversation about the house on Fairlawn Street.

"I understand all that, Dee. I just want you to take a look now that I've made a few changes and cleaned things up a bit more. Honestly, I haven't seen or felt any, you know, *presence* there. Not since the night of the sé-ance. Let's put all that stuff behind us and try to look at the place with fresh eyes. Then we'll decide together."

Sam put his last bitc of pizza into his mouth and then talked around it. "But if we *do* put the house back on the market I'm going with a different realtor. Bob's had his chance." And God forbid that Bob should mention Amber's offer to Dee.

He swallowed and went on. "And I'm not staying in the old apartment at the rates they want now, especially since you don't like it. If we don't move to Fairlawn Street we're going to have to do some apartment shopping really soon to be out of there by New Year."

Dee thought about how the leasing agent had tried to pressure her into signing a lease on a new apartment. She hadn't told Sam she'd been apartment hunting, and didn't plan to. She sighed. "How did everything get so complicated?"

"Both of us have been going through a lot. But at least we're together." He reached for her hand. "What do you say? Are you about ready to go?"

"One more trip to the bathroom, and then I'm ready."

They drove the three blocks to the house and pulled in the drive. "Did you leave the lights on?" Dee asked.

Sam's brow furrowed. "I don't think so. Maybe Bob was here again."

They sat in the driveway while the garage door creaked its way up. It was a cloudless, frosty night. "The place looks nice," Sam said, trying to sound encouraging. "Kind of inviting, don't you think?" Warm light glowed from the dining room and through the sidelights at the front door. A pair of handsome carriage lights illuminated the small front porch.

"Yeah. It does look inviting." Dee slid down in her seat. "But I'm still nervous."

"Don't worry. If things go badly, we're leaving. That's it." He wore a look of grim resolve as he walked around the car and opened her door. "Let's go in through the front. We'll look at the house from a buyer's perspective."

As they went up the sidewalk Dee glanced sideways into the dining room. This time everything was still, but the sight of the window blinds made her shiver. "Make sure the coast is clear," she said. "If you see anyone I'm not going in."

Sam nodded. He slid his key into the lock, stepped into the foyer, and walked slowly through the house.

Birdie emerged in the entryway, a ghostly mist that kept out of sight hovering near the ceiling. "A groom should carry his bride over the threshold," she whispered.

Dee closed her eyes and took a steadying breath. In that instant she remembered the bridal gown from Birdie's closet. She imagined herself in a sweeping veil being lifted in her groom's arms and carried into the house. It brought a smile to her face. "Maybe before I gained these twenty-five pounds," she thought.

"All clear," Sam said, taking her hand and leading Dee inside.

She stopped where she was and looked around the silent foyer. The space felt very neutral. A part of her wished she had Maureen's sensitivity to spirits. She wished she knew whether she and Sam were actually alone.

"Maybe a picture, or a mirror above that console there. The mirror from the second bedroom in the apartment would work," she said. She held up a hand to stop the comment that hovered on Sam's lips. "Just some staging ideas. Let's not get ahead of ourselves."

The living room appeared almost empty. All that remained of his parents' furnishings there was the couch that they agreed was so comfortable.

She peered nervously into the dining room where the table and the old hutch remained. Her shoulders relaxed. "I love this old-style furniture," she remarked.

"Thirty-five years old, and still looks new," Birdie murmured. Sam looked up sharply, but his mother now hid from sight in the foyer.

"I guess it's old-fashioned," Dee said. "You don't see it much anymore, but it just says 'family gathering' to me. And that's just it. I want to have my sisters over to visit, and my parents and my brothers, when they're in town. But I know Mo won't come to a haunted house! Can you guarantee that your parents are gone, and will stay gone?"

Sam looked into Dee's eyes, and then shifted his gaze a few inches higher. Birdie floated behind Dee, emphatically nodding her head up and down.

"I can guarantee that you'll never be bothered by ghosts," he said. "And none of your family will be bothered either." He gave his mother a commanding stare. Birdie rolled her eyes.

They continued through the house. Dee was delighted with the changes Sam had made in the kitchen, especially the new light fixtures. "It's been awful cooking in the apartment because we're always standing in a shadow," Sam said. "See how bright it is now?"

Birdie darted away just in time as Sam and Dee looked up toward the ceiling.

The other two rooms and the second bathroom were largely untouched. Dee lingered at the doorway to Sam's old bedroom. "This would be the nursery," she said, and then gave Sam a stern look. "*If* we move here." Her heart melted at the hopeful expression on his face. "You and your puppy-dog eyes," she said, and gave him a peck on the cheek.

"Okay, the master suite is going to make or break the deal. Let's go." Dee led the way this time, back through the house and down the short hall. Sam followed, with Birdie floating along at the end of the procession. Sam saw her out of the corner of his eye, and turned to shake a fist at her.

Dee stopped at the threshold of the bedroom and clapped her hands lightly together. "Oh! I like it!"

"Yeah, the stuff you ordered for the bed looks great with the new wall color," Sam agreed, his shoulders relaxing.

"It's calming, like a spa place, or one of those fancy hotel rooms," Birdie said from inside a closet.

"It's so soothing," Dee said. "It's like a picture out of a magazine, isn't it? I knew the blinds and the woodwork would be fine as is, but I wasn't sure about the carpet. It definitely works, though."

"And look," Sam said. "There was tile in the bathroom after all, and it's in great shape. All we had to do was rip up that old carpet and toss it."

The bathroom carpet was the only thing Birdie and Martin ever argued about. And now it was gone. Birdie wore a satisfied smile, peeking out from the closet as Deidre slowly scanned the room.

Dee's eyes lingered on the new bedcovers.

"That bed sure looks comfortable," Birdie suggested gliding away down the hall.

Deidre turned to Sam with a shy smile and reached for his hand, pulling him toward the bed. "Maybe we should try it out, just to be sure."

Chapter 23

Dee watched from the dining room window as Sam tried again and again to back the U-Haul up the driveway, veering more than once onto the frozen lawn. Birdie watched too, hovering near the ceiling and clicking her tongue.

Finally Dee couldn't stand it anymore. She ran out the front door and flagged him down. "Just park it on the street and bring things in through the front door. It's wider than the door in the garage anyway." She ran back in with a shiver, wrapping her sweater more tightly around her.

Sam gave her an irritated look but wisely refrained from saying anything. For the past week Sam and Dee had sorted through their belongings and packed things into boxes. He had hired his friend Chris, and Brad, another guy from work, to help move everything. More quickly than he'd thought possible they had crammed his little bit of furniture and all their boxes into the truck. Now they were at the house on Fairlawn Street to unload it all and move in.

Dee's sister Trish was ready to be put to work, dressed in sweats and sneakers with her blonde hair in a messy knot on top of her head. As soon as Sam and the guys moved the suitcases and boxes full of clothes into the bedroom, the two women began filling up the dresser and hanging shirts, pants, skirts, and dresses in the closets.

"Guess what I bought the other day," Dee told Trish, not waiting for an answer. "Some of those under-the-bed storage bins. Since the closets aren't the biggest, I figured I could make room by putting out-of-season stuff under the bed."

"Out-of-season, and stuff you won't be fitting into for a while," Trish said with a grin.

"That too," Dee agreed. "Slide that cardboard box over here. It's full of summer stuff, and it's all going straight into the bins."

Trish finished hanging Sam's clothes, and opened the door to Dee's closet. "What's this in the garment bag?"

"Didn't I tell you?" Dee said, suspended in the act of shoving underwear into a drawer. "It's Birdie Ebersole's wedding dress. Can you believe it? It's like – thirty-five years old, but it's in great shape."

"Vintage! What are you going to do with it?" Trish asked. "Some people have them remade into christening gowns and things."

"Yeah, I've thought of that, but I'd kind of hate to cut it up." She hesitated. "I'm wondering if I could, you know …"

"Could what?" Trish looked curiously at her sister.

"Could wear it."

Trish's eyes widened. "Don't tell me. Is my career-minded little sister actually thinking of getting married and settling down?"

"You say it like it's a bad thing," Dee said laughing. Then she turned serious. "You know, I never intended to get pregnant so soon after finishing college. I feel like I'm doing everything backwards. Start a family, *then* find a place to live, and *then* get married. I don't know what I want anymore. Maybe it's just all the hormones." She tried to smile but then sat on the bed and unexpectedly started to cry.

"Hey!" Trish sat next to her and patted Dee's knee. "Nothing to cry about here! You've got a cute, cute house, and a guy who's crazy about you. What else could you ask?"

Dee sniffed. She wrestled a tissue out of the pocket of her maternity jeans and dabbed at her face. "I know. And I'm feeling good about all that. It's just – a lot at once, you know? And I'm too young to settle down! My life is going seriously off-script. Work has been picking up. I managed to get some good gigs. But ever since this –" she pointed at her growing belly "and seeing this house, all I want to do is stay home and be a mommy." She wailed, and started crying again. "That's so not me!"

"It's probably that nesting instinct, or whatever. Wait until the baby starts screaming. You might feel different then." Trish's face softened. "Then again, maybe it *is* you, and you just didn't know it until now. Being a mom for a while might be just the thing for you, at least until the kids are in school."

"*Kids!*" Dee said with alarm. "What are you trying to say? I think the doctor would have told me by now if I were carrying twins!"

"I'm just saying the women in our family tend to be really fertile."

"Boy, I've got to get that under control in a hurry," Dee said, and then added, "I thought I *had* it under control. Was I ever wrong!"

"Little sis, what makes you think we're ever in control?" Trish said, and gave her sister a hug.

Birdie Ebersole smiled from her perch on the armchair near the window.

Chapter 24

"Hey, man. Brad needs to get home, and we need to turn in that truck," Chris said. Sam and his friends had arranged what little furniture there was as best they could, and had stacked the last of the boxes in the front entryway.

"Okay. Let me tell Dee, and then we'll be on our way." Sam grabbed a box with the word 'bathroom' scrawled on it and headed to the master suite. He found Dee and Trish still working in the bedroom.

"We're going to go return the truck," he said, setting the box down. "Everything okay back here?" He noticed Dee looked flushed. "You're not overdoing it, are you?" He reached out and gently tucked a lock of hair behind her ear.

"I'm fine. We're getting a lot done. Tell the guys how much we appreciated their help." Dee placed her hand over Sam's and forced a smile. "Hey, and pick us up some lunch while you're out. We're going to have to go to the grocery store one of these days."

Sam nodded and returned to the dining room, patting his pocket to make sure he hadn't mislaid the keys. "Okay, guys, let's go." Outside a few snowflakes drifted through the air, collecting along the edge of the sidewalk.

The three men piled into the front seat of the U-haul. "We really appreciate your help," Sam said. "It didn't take nearly as long as I thought to get our stuff moved. It may take a while to get all the boxes squared away, but – that's moving for you."

"Speaking of boxes, I never saw a box for a Christmas tree," Chris said.

"Christmas tree?" Sam gave him a blank look. "I don't have a tree or any of that stuff. Dee doesn't either."

Chris gave him a stern look "And I feel it's my duty to point out your deficiency in that department. You *got* to have a Christmas tree if you're gonna start out right in that new home of yours. You know, to keep the little woman happy. Trust me on this."

"You know all about keeping women happy, do you?" Sam asked, eyebrows raised. It occurred to him he knew little about Chris's private life. He certainly didn't recall him mentioning anyone special. It seemed like the guy was too busy working all the time.

At the other end of the bench seat Brad chuckled. "Chris and his *woman* have six kids," he said. "He must be doin' something she likes!"

Sam stared at Chris before returning his eyes to the road. "Six! Were they all conceived during the Christmas holidays, or something?"

Chris held his hand up to put a stop to the idle talk. "No, it's ... What can I say? I love that woman! And I like kids. I do take care of their Christmas decorating needs, though. I like to make it nice for them. Making memories, and all that. You know, they're only young once."

Sam breathed a big sigh. "Well, Chris, all the extra cash I have right now is earmarked for paying you and Brad to help us move. And to tell the truth, I've been ignoring the hints Dee has dropped about putting up a tree. So what do you suggest?"

"Here's what I've been trying to say, if Brad would quit jabbering and hold his peace. Someone donated a Christmas tree and a box full of decorations to the food bank. We already have a tree we set up in the lobby, so I thought you might like this one. It's not new, but the lights work. We checked it out yesterday."

Sam pulled into the U-Haul lot in silence, and was momentarily busy returning the rental. Out in the parking lot he paid his two helpers and Brad took off in his old clunker.

Sam and Chris walked to Sam's truck. "This'll be the first Christmas without my parents," Sam said, thinking aloud. It was like having a sore thumb. He would forget the pain of his loss, only for it to return with a sharp stab at odd times – like this one. He remembered the tired look on Dee's face earlier, and wondered if a tree would perk her up. Maybe it would cheer them *both* up.

"Okay. Let's go check out this tree of yours."

He knew the perfect spot in the living room for a Christmas tree, the same spot next to the fireplace where his family's tree had stood all those years. He had no idea what had become of their old tree. It probably ended up at the thrift store after Dee's sisters cleaned out the house. He didn't know what-all they had been up to while he was painting. If he hadn't caught them in time, they'd have given away the tools from his dad's old workshop out in the garage.

There were reasons Sam didn't have his own tree, and it wasn't just because he had been living in a small apartment. There was something stressful about Christmas, Sam thought. Apparently his mother had thought so too, because every year when they had decorated their tree an anxious feeling hung over the house, a feeling that couldn't be dispelled even when his mother talked in a cheery voice and turned up the volume on the Christmas carols playing on the stereo. There was always something forced about it.

Sam unlocked the door at Gracious Plenty Food Bank and Chris led him to a storage closet. Together they dragged a couple of boxes out into the warehouse. Chris dug inside the larger box and pulled the end of a power cord toward an electrical outlet, plugging it in. Colored lights flared to life in the box. "See? Doesn't that just lift your spirits?"

"Can you help me load this stuff into my truck?" Sam asked. "That would lift my spirits."

"Better than that. I can help you set everything up. *If* lunch is included."

After a quick trip through the drive-thru at a local restaurant, Sam parked his truck in front of the house on Fairlawn Street. The snow had stopped, leaving a white frosting on the grass.

Sam ran into the house with containers of food for Dee and Trish. He found them taking a break in the office where Dee had been setting up her computer gear. Her laptop and a monitor were arranged on the worktable and a small printer was on the floor. "Hey, stay back here for a few minutes. We're working on something in the living room."

"Stay back here?" Dee asked. She looked at Trish, who put her hands on her hips.

"I mean, you can go into the kitchen, but stay out of the living room." He gave her a wink.

Dee shook her head with a resigned smile. "We won't come in until you call us. But don't do anything that can't be undone!"

"If only we had one of those drones that sends pictures to your phone," Trish whispered. "We could fly it into the living room and spy on them."

"Maybe you should buy me one for Christmas," Dee agreed.

Chapter 25

Birdie didn't need a drone for spying. A gray mist darting back and forth across the living room ceiling, she kept out of sight and watched the two men. If she still had an actual stomach, she was sure she would be feeling butterflies right now. She had always stressed over Christmas, wanting to make it perfect for her family, and always feeling like a failure.

She wondered why that was. Another example of trying to meet impossible standards set by the TV programs she had watched and magazines she had read?

Sam felt nervous too as he ran to the truck and dragged in the box full of ornaments. Was he doing the same thing his mother had done? Forced gaiety around decorating for the holidays?

He tried to remember what Christmas was like at Dee's house when they were both kids. He hadn't been included in any of their celebrations, but he spent time there with her brothers during the school holidays. He remembered a tree in the corner of their living room, and playing board games around the dining room table, and always lots of cookies. He didn't remember feeling stressed about anything.

Chris had already brought in the box with the tree. "Come on. Let's see how quick we can get this put together," Sam said.

"I'm an expert at this kind," Chris bragged. "I've set them up before."

It didn't look very complicated, considering the tree was in only two parts. Sam watched as the expert put it together and stood it in the built-in stand. He plugged it in next to the fireplace, and Sam began to rummage in the other box for ornaments.

"No, no, no!" Chris said. "You have to let the women decorate it, or at least let them tell you where to put the stuff on the tree. Don't you know anything?"

Sam rolled his eyes. "Chris, you are a life-saver. I was about to blow it." He disappeared down the hall, and returned to the living room with Dee and Trish trailing behind him.

One look at the tree and both women shrieked and started laughing. "Right after you left we thought about putting up the tree and surprising you," Dee said. She put her arms round Sam. "You had a sad look on your face earlier. I wanted to cheer you up." She pulled him into a warm hug.

"Wait a minute," Sam leaned back, wide-eyed. "Where were you going to get a Christmas tree from?"

"Your parents' tree!" Dee looked surprised that he'd asked. "Isn't this it? From the attic over the garage? Trish saw it the day we cleared stuff out. I knew we didn't have one, so I told her to leave it up there."

Sam bolted for the garage while Chris explained, "We picked this one up from the food bank. Someone donated it, but we didn't need it."

"You could always put up two trees," Trish suggested. "One on either side of the fireplace."

"Yes!" Dee exclaimed, clapping her hands.

With a big smile Chris went to help bring things in from the garage.

"I thought all this got donated to the thrift shop," Sam said, pushing a stack of boxes into the room.

"No way! I love this kind of stuff. As my siblings got older and moved away I was the one left home to do all the decorating. Mom gave me free rein. I used to crank up the Christmas music on the CD player and go to town." Dee pulled her cell phone out of her pocket, and soon holiday tunes resonated through the house. "Come on! Set up this tree so we can get to work!"

Sam opened the box and stared into it, bewildered.

"Stand aside," Chris said. "Let the expert do the job." The tree was in more pieces than the first, but Chris still had it up in record time. "Now the rest of you can get started on the fun part."

As Dee and Trish pulled strings of beaded garland out of one box, Sam dug in another, with cries of recognition at ornaments that had decorated his family's tree over the years.

There was a sharp knock on the front door, and a second later Maureen walked in followed by her two kids. "We came to see how everything is going. I brought some of my chia balls, because I know you've been eating nothing but junk food all day."

"Chia balls!" Chad pulled a face.

"They're not for you, kiddo. Hey, DeeDee, you know your doorbell still doesn't work."

"If you buy a new one I can hook it up," Chris told Sam.

"I'm sure you can," Sam said with a smile.

Caitlyn jumped up and down. "Two trees! Mom, how come they get to have two trees and we haven't even put ours up yet? Can we have two trees this year?"

"No! But I bet Aunt DeeDee will let you help decorate hers." She bent to peer into a box of ornaments. "Where did you get all this fun stuff?"

The twinkling lights and glittering baubles soon transformed the living room as kids and adults dug ornaments out of boxes and arranged them on the trees in a joyful holiday frenzy. Even Chris couldn't resist getting in on the fun, until he was summoned by the mother of his children. "Duty calls," he said to Sam. "I'm needed to set up another Christmas tree. I hope you can give me a ride across town."

Sam looked from one to the other, and then placed the angel on top of his parents' old Christmas tree.

"It's like you have an elf on the shelf watching over everything," Caitlyn said.

Maureen glanced at Sam and then quickly looked away.

Sam smiled. "Yep. We have our own Christmas angel watching over us."

* * *

After the merriment wound down and all the helpers scattered to their own homes, Sam and Dee made their way to the master suite to try out the shower.

Birdie drifted into the garage and leaned against the workbench next to Martin's old recliner. "You'll never guess, Martin. They've put up two Christmas trees!"

The sparkle in her eyes made Martin grin. "Did they use all the old ornaments?"

"Yes. And the manger scene is on the mantel like always. And that cute little girl was here, with her brother this time. And there was music in the house. It felt so alive! Oh, Martin!" She flew back to the living room, a filmy mist hovering near the ceiling, and gazed enraptured, lost in the beauty of the colorful twinkling lights.

Chapter 27

One Saturday morning a few months later Dee danced with delight in a very pregnant sort of way while Sam, Maureen, and her husband Ryan looked on. "I love it! It's perfect!" she said, running her fingers over the rail of the crib they had just set up in the small bedroom.

"Keep it as long as you need it. We don't expect to have a baby again any time soon." Maureen smiled and held up crossed fingers.

"I'll go bring in the box with the sheets and stuff," Ryan said, and headed for the garage followed by Sam.

"Thanks." Dee nodded. "I want to have everything ready before this baby decides to show up." She rubbed the side of her belly, wincing slightly. Sam's old dresser was packed with new clothes, diapers, and other things for the baby. His old bookcase was crowded with toys, and his little desk had been moved out to make room for a changing table.

Maureen looked at the sky-blue walls. "Do you think you'll have a boy?"

"Don't know, don't care," Dee said. "After all the hassle of moving, we just didn't feel like painting another room." She picked up a plush toy from the rocking chair that had been moved in from the master bedroom.

The guys came back carrying two boxes. "Here's the box that goes with the crib," Ryan said.

"I brought sheets, changing pads, and a few blankets," Maureen said. "I threw in some bibs that weren't too messed up, but you won't need those for a while."

"I found this other box out there," Sam said. "I thought it was just something of mine, but it looks like bathing suits and pool towels."

"Oh, good. I wondered where that stuff went. Will you put it in the bedroom, and I'll deal with it later?" Dee said.

Ryan glanced out the back window. "Oh for Pete's sake." He tapped on the glass and shouted, "Get out of the dirt! Caitlyn! Chad! What is it with these kids?" He went outside to rescue the garden.

Maureen rummaged in the box and pulled out a couple of sheets, choosing one to cover the crib mattress. "It seems pretty quiet around here," she said.

"Quiet?"

"As in, I don't sense any apparitions – any visitors from *the beyond*." Her voice took on that spooky quality again.

"Thank God. Sam says they've stayed away. I'm glad to know you're not feeling anything. Maybe they finally *crossed over*. The last thing I want is to have to deal with ghosts while I'm trying to breastfeed."

"Darn it, that reminds me. I've got a couple of those blouses at home that have slits in the sides, you know, so you can stick the baby's head in to nurse. You might like to try them. I'll bring them next time. I do think you're going to need them sooner rather than later."

"I hope you're right," Dee said rubbing her belly again. "I'm looking forward to it being *over*. Baby feels like it's stuck in there." She giggled nervously.

"You can handle it. Sam will be with you. I've told mom she is *not* to come smother you, but she'll come to help whenever you want. She can stay at Trish's apartment. And I'm just a phone call away."

"Thanks. It's so nice to have family I can count on."

"It is," Maureen agreed. "Poor Sam. He doesn't have anyone."

"He's got an aunt and uncle and some cousins who are really nice. And he's got all of us," Dee added.

"And baby makes three!" Maureen tucked in the last corner of the sheet and gave the crib a pat. "Let's go see what my kids are up to. By now they've probably buried their dad in the back yard."

The women left the nursery, and a misty shadow slowly descended from a corner near the ceiling. Birdie materialized and leaned over the crib to run her hand over the soft sheet. She smiled faintly as she faded again and disappeared.

Chapter 28

Sam's phone rang just as he got to the master bedroom with the box. He set it on the bed and glanced at his phone to see who was calling.

"Hi, Chris. What's up?"

"Have I got a deal for you, and it'll only take a little while out of your Saturday," Chris said with excitement in his voice. "What would you say to a whole truckload of free food?"

"You know what I'd say. I never turn anything down. Where's this truckload coming from?" Normally food deliveries and distribution to local food pantries happened during the week.

"Baby-mama's cousin works in the office at Fortress Foods. One of their reefer trucks broke down in transit. Well, they got the truck fixed, and the food's still good, but they can't get it across country by the delivery deadline. It's going to the landfill if they can't do something with it quick. What do you say?"

Sam was always energized by opportunities like this. Grocery stores were in the business of selling food, not giving it away. But Sam and his predecessors had shown them how they could better manage their inventory and deal with their surpluses. And a myriad of partner organizations was waiting to pass the food along to those in need, keeping it out of the landfill.

"I'm trying to think if we have room for it all, or should contact some of our partners to pick it up." Sam mentally flipped through the food pantries, after-school programs, and soup kitchens in the counties served by Gracious Plenty.

"Me and Brad been working out space in the warehouse. I don't think it'll be a problem. All we need is some paperwork from you to make Fortress happy, if you can come in for a few minutes."

Sam told Chris he'd be right in, and went to tell Dee.

"On a Saturday?" Dee asked.

"Yeah, I got a call from Chris about a truckload of perishables that we can have if we act fast. They're making room at the food bank, but I need to get some paperwork together, contact the food pantries that'll be open early in the week, and talk to the people that run the mobile food store. Hopefully I won't be gone long. Will you be all right? We could ask Maureen to stay."

"I'll be fine. Go ahead and go. I might work on that new project for a while, although I'd really like to take a nap. Besides, Trish said she'd drop over later. I'm going to put her to work moving some things around in the office."

"Okay," Sam said. He placed his arm around Dee's shoulder and they watched from the driveway while Maureen eased her mini-van around a utility truck parked across the street. As soon as she drove off Sam started his old pick-up. He rolled down the window and leaned out. "Just call me if … You know, if you need any-thing."

"Don't worry. I'm fine! I'm sure I can nap by myself! This might be my last chance. Call me when you guys fin-ish up. Maybe I'll make dinner." She blew him a kiss. "Or order dinner," she said under her breath, waving him off.

Dee returned to the house and glanced in her office next to the nursery. She had started on a job for a new client, and had made good progress. She hoped to finish it before baby interrupted, and with the house quiet maybe now would be a good time to work for an hour or two.

A big yawn changed her mind. If she got a nap in be-fore Trish showed up, she could get some work done later that afternoon, when she didn't feel so sleepy.

She took one more look in the nursery and then went to her bedroom where the box of swimsuits and things waited on the bed. She lifted out the pool towels and tossed them haphazardly on the bottom shelf of the small linen closet in the bathroom.

Then she dumped the remaining contents of the box on the bed. There was a cover-up and two old bathing suits that she hoped she would fit into again come summer.

She smiled, remembering summer afternoons at the public swimming pool back when her family still lived on Fairlawn Street. She was sorry she'd missed out on watching Sam when he was on the swim team in high school and then in college. He still loved to swim, and had the toned body to show for it.

Awkwardly she knelt down and slid one of the bins out from under the bed. With difficulty she pried the lid off and stuffed the bathing suits inside. Then she snapped the lid shut and slid it under the bed. "Now comes the hard part. Getting back up."

She sat sideways on one hip contemplating getting up. "Maureen was right, this carpet really is soft. Thank you, Martin Ebersole, for the extra padding." She lay down on her side on the carpet, folding one arm under her head like a pillow. A moment later, she was asleep.

* * *

Birdie materialized again in Samuel's old bedroom glancing with approval at the crib. She couldn't wait for the baby to come. It wouldn't be long now.

She floated through the house, visiting each room like a silent benediction. She was so pleased at all the new life there, both inside and out. She gazed out the window, watching as the shade cast by the trees crept up the lawn. Early spring showers had caused the yard to green up and the trees to start leafing out. Yes, Dee's baby was coming at a good time.

The thought of Dee made Birdie wonder where she was. She often kept a protective watch, always making sure to keep out of sight. Now she realized she hadn't seen or heard her in a while.

She did another tour past the office and through the kitchen. She scanned the living and dining rooms. She zoomed to the master bedroom heading for the ensuite bathroom.

That's when she saw Dee on the floor. She was on her side, perfectly still.

Birdie moaned, a drawn out, painful wail. She cried out a second time, but this time her wail was cut short by a pounding on the front door.

Trish knocked, and peered into the entryway through the sidelights. She pressed the useless doorbell, cursing under her breath when she realized it was still out of order, and hammered louder.

Birdie sped through the door and whirled around the woman, whipping up a small cyclone. "Dee needs help!

She's on the floor in the bedroom!" she shouted. Frantically she made another circuit but Trish was oblivious to Birdie's presence. She tucked a lock of windblown blond hair behind her ear, and fished in her purse for her cell phone.

"What the hell's wrong with you? Are you deaf? Dee is in trouble!" Birdie shouted again. She looked around for some way to get Trish's attention. Then she remembered what little Caitlyn had said about a ghost in a movie breaking light bulbs.

"This had better work," Birdie said. She clenched her jaw and both fists, and closed her eyes tightly. Suddenly the light bulbs in the carriage lights on either side of the front door exploded with a loud pop, showering bits of glass over the small porch.

Trish stepped back with a startled yelp. She stared up at the broken fixtures, then looked behind her where the utility truck was still parked across the street. "Hey!" she shouted, marching across the lawn to confront the crew standing at the base of the light pole.

"It wasn't them! Trish, come back! Oh, why did it have to be you?" Birdie groaned. Trish never did seem to sense when Birdie was around.

She returned to the bedroom where Dee was still lying on the floor. A sick feeling swirled where her stomach used to be. "I have to get to Samuel! I have to!" She hovered over the young woman for an agonizing moment. Then she closed her eyes tightly, rose through the ceiling and disappeared.

Chapter 29

Trish gave the utility workers a dressing down, even though they insisted nothing they were working on would have shattered the porch lights. "They don't just explode on their own, you know. I wouldn't be surprised if you fried the wiring in the whole house. Your main office is going to hear about this," she said, breathing hard as she marched back across the front yard.

She pulled out her cell phone and called Dee's number. "Where are you? I've been on your front porch for half an hour," Trish said.

"I fell asleep," Dee said. "I was exhausted. This people-making business takes a lot out of you, and I've been kind of achy since yesterday." Trish could hear her sister grunt as she got up, and watched through the sidelights until she finally opened the front door.

"What happened out here!" Dee asked, seeing the shattered glass on the porch.

"Those butt-holes across the street are trying to blow up the neighborhood. You'd better check if your power is working," Trish said.

"Let's go into the office. I need your help in there any-way." Dee led the way to the other side of the house, still holding her cell phone in her hand, talking as she went. "Since I told Uncle Ed I won't be coming in to work at Walsh anymore, he told me to just take the monitor home. That was nice of him. I've got it hooked up, but I need to move some other stuff around."

She flipped the light switch in the office and the over-head fixture came on. "So far, so good." Then she plugged her phone into the charger that lay on the desk. The battery icon illuminated, and she heard the little tone indicating the phone was charging. "Seems to be okay here. By the way, take a look in the nursery. Mo and Ryan set up the crib for me today."

Trish gave her nod of approval to the nursery, and then the two women set about making some adjustments to the office. Dee planned to work from home after the baby arrived, assuming the little one ever took a nap. Her business had been even more successful than she hoped.

"I'd like to move the printer over to this little table," Dee said. "Then I can slide the other monitor over and have more room for the keyboard."

"Okay. What are all these stacks of paper?" Trish asked.

"Careful with that. It's all the stuff Sammy's been deal-ing with. He's still settling his parents' estate, and has to file their income tax. It's taking forever to get everything done, but – I guess it's kind of like having a baby. Not something you can rush."

The two women cleared everything off the little table. "Okay, now for the printer."

"Let me get it," Trish said.

"Oh, get real. It's just a printer and it's not moving that far. You and Sammy think I'm going to break or something." Dee grabbed the printer but before she could set it on the table her expression changed. "Uh-oh. *Quick!* Quick, get a towel or something!"

"Oh, boy," Trish said, running to the hall bathroom for a towel. She handed it to Dee and relieved her of the hardware.

"Darn it. These are my most comfortable maternity pants. Now they're all yucky." Dee tried to say it as a joke but her shaky voice and the look on her face betrayed her anxiety.

"Come on, let's get you into something dry. I think it's time we took a little trip to City Hospital." Dee stood frozen, still looking helpless. "I'm a nurse, remember? You have nothing to worry about." Trish took hold of Dee's arm and Dee waddled along with the towel still stuffed between her legs as her sister gently led her through the house.

"Come on, DeeDee. Where are your clean clothes? And where's your go-bag? You told me you had it all packed."

Dee rummaged in her drawers and pulled out some pants and underwear, then disappeared into the bathroom. She could hear Trish on the phone to the obstetrician's office.

Dee reappeared, holding her soiled clothes in her hand. "Oh, just drop those in the shower stall. We don't have time to worry about laundry. Sam can take care of that later."

"Sammy!" Dee cried. "We have to call him."

"We'll call him from the car! Look, girly. I'm a nurse, but not in obstetrics. I'd rather have someone besides me deliver your baby, so speed it up a little and let's go."

Chapter 30

Birdie was completely disoriented. She felt like she was moving, but had no sense of direction, and couldn't remember where she was going.

She opened her eyes to find herself in a space of dark nothingness. She had the uncomfortable sensation of being squeezed, like a tube of toothpaste being grasped in the middle. She didn't know if she was going toward the cap end, or down to the bottom of the tube. It made her feel sick, so she closed her eyes again, trying to remember.

She was on vacation. She was riding on a bus. She was on her way to somewhere important. Someone needed her help. Was it Martin?

Where had she seen him last? In his recliner, she was sure. He was always there. She took comfort in that. She loved having Martin around. Martin who had rescued her.

Thoughts and memories paraded through her mind competing for attention. She was buying a wedding gown. No one was more surprised than herself. After all, she was not anyone's first choice for a prom date. She just wasn't that cute. Too serious. Four-eyed. Sharp-tongued. When she threw herself into her work and called herself career-minded it was partly in self-defense, so she didn't have to admit how awful it felt to be passed over and left behind while all her friends were having bridal showers and then baby showers and getting on with their lives.

And then she'd met Martin, just a chance encounter at one of those boring chamber of commerce luncheons. He was kind and thoughtful. He had nice manners and those warm brown eyes. Somehow he'd seen something in her. Something that he liked. He supported her, and respected her ability and ambition.

She was on her way to do something important. She had to get to work. But no, she had just retired.

She was going somewhere. She was riding on a bus headed home, and then ... Then she remembered. She was dead. She had seen the urns on the mantel. The mantel of the house that she'd shared with Martin. And Samuel.

She missed her son. She wanted to talk to Samuel. She needed to tell him something.

Birdie's eyes flew open again. She needed to talk to Samuel.

She struggled, feeling stuck, like she was wedged in that tube of toothpaste, not moving. "Damn it, I have to get out!" she shouted.

Suddenly it was as if the cap at the end of the tube flew off, and she was moving, being drawn outward. A feeling of exhilaration took hold of her. She was moving!

She looked in the direction she was heading and gasped. "My God! It's beautiful!" Showers of golden stars, more radiant and glittering than the prettiest fireworks she'd ever seen, were visible though the opening ahead of her.

A yearning welled up inside her, starting deep in the soles of her feet and filling her to the top of her head. She wanted desperately to get closer to the golden light. It was warm and compelling, full of energy. She wanted to be part of that light more than anything she had ever desired in her life.

"Yes," she whispered. "I'm coming."

Something held her, something painful. She felt stretched, like she was on a torture device that threatened to pull her apart. She dragged her eyes away from the glorious light and clenched them tightly closed.

"No! I have to talk to Samuel. Dee's in trouble. Samuel!" A sickening whirling took hold of her again and she screamed, careening into the darkness.

* * *

At his desk at work Sam felt uneasy. He wondered if he should call Dee, but he knew she hadn't slept well the night before, and he hated to disturb her if she was napping.

He'd finished the paperwork the food distributor needed and gave it to the truck driver, who had helped oversee the unloading. Chris and the other guys had handled the rest, and had already said their goodbyes.

Sam had spent the next hour phoning and texting contacts in local food pantries, soup kitchens, and an after-school program, and was pleased that all the extra food Chris had got them was now spoken for.

Chris was a marvel. Sam pondered how he could move him up the ladder at Gracious Plenty, to get him more hours and higher pay. He certainly deserved it.

Suddenly Sam stiffened. Goosebumps rose up over his whole body. He looked around the tiny office, eyes wide, listening. The building was deserted, but he could have sworn he'd heard someone call his name.

It sounded like his mother.

Was it possible? Wasn't she somehow bound to the house? How on earth could she reach him here? And why?

Sam got up from his desk and thrust his head out the door of the little office. It was quiet in the warehouse.

His goosebumps turned into a prickling, warm sensation. It was suddenly too hot in the office. Maybe it was time he called it a day. All he had to do was finish the email he was working on, and he could go home.

He sat back down at his desk, but the urge to call Dee *right now* wouldn't leave him. He tapped on his cell phone and waited an agonizingly long time as her phone rang and rang and then went to voicemail.

He thumbed through his contacts looking for a number for Maureen or Trish. Suddenly a gust of wind lifted the papers off his desk and scattered them to the floor, and there in front of him was his mother, full of light and glowing fiercely, her hair flying around her face. He rolled back from the desk and jumped out of his chair. His phone fell clattering into a corner.

"Dee needs you!" Birdie said, her voice shrill and demanding.

"Ma! How did you get here? What happened? What did you do?"

"I didn't do anything! I found her on the floor. I don't know if she's dead or alive. What the hell are you waiting for?"

His phone buzzed and flashed in the corner and he quickly retrieved it, groaning when he saw Trish's name. His hands shook as he swiped at the screen.

"Hey, it's me." Dee's voice over the phone flooded Sam with relief. "Get ready to meet your child. We're on our way to the hospital."

His knees felt wobbly. He groped for his chair and sat down. "I'm coming! Are you all right? Are you driving?!"

"Chill, first-time-dad!" Sam heard Trish's voice coming from the other side of the car. "I'm driving, and everything's under control. But it won't be long now."

"What happened? I tried to call you." Sam ran a shaky hand through his hair, glancing at his mother while he listened.

"I'm having contractions and my water just broke. We left in a hurry and I forgot my phone was charging."

"There's nothing to worry about," Trish added. "So don't get any speeding tickets. Just meet us at the hospital, okay?"

"Right. I'll be right there." He jabbed at the phone, his hands still trembling, and looked up at his mother.

"What's happening?" Birdie asked.

"Trish is driving Dee to the hospital. Dee's water broke, but everything's under control. You scared me half to death, Ma!"

"You! I was scared half to death. And I'm already there!" Maybe she wasn't already there. Birdie remembered the space of dark nothingness, and yearned momentarily for the place with the golden starlight.

She wondered if she could get back to the house on Fairlawn. She was half afraid she would wind up somewhere else.

Sam hastily gathered things up. He scribbled a note and then made a quick phone call, explaining to someone on the other end that he was on his way to the hospital.

"Samuel, you have to take me with you," Birdie said.

"With me? What, like drive you to the hospital?"

"Please! Don't ask me any questions, just do it."

He growled. "Oh, Ma! I don't know how this is supposed to work, but – come on."

Chapter 31

Sam dashed out to his truck and climbed in the driver's seat. When he looked up from buckling his seatbelt his mother was there next to him. "This is so weird," he muttered. "Ma, I thought you promised to stay out of the way and not watch us all the time. What were you doing? Spying on Dee?"

"No! Not spying. Oh, Samuel. I guess I miss being alive. I miss having our little family at our house. I was so excited when Maureen brought that crib over today. I just had to peek in the nursery. Then I did a quick walk-through of the house. That's when I saw Dee on the floor, in the bedroom. I got really scared."

"Okay. Well, thanks Ma, for coming to get me, I guess."

"I've been so looking forward to this baby," Birdie said. "I can't tell you."

"I hope the baby makes you happier than I did," Sam said a little sourly.

"What?" Birdie's voice rose. "Samuel, why would you say a thing like that? I loved you! And you were a great kid!"

Sam looked at his mother. "Then why do I sometimes have the feeling that you weren't that happy with me? That I wasn't *enough*?"

"Samuel, I was thrilled with you! I've told you, I loved being your mom. I'm sorry if I put pressure on you, or made you feel like you weren't living up to some ideal, or weren't enough. You were great just the way you were. What I really wished was that I'd had *more* kids. That's the only way I didn't have enough."

"More kids? Ma, I thought I was an accident! I mean, face it. You weren't young when you had me. They call that a geriatric pregnancy, according to our childbirth training."

"Yeah, well I wasn't a spring chicken when I got married, either. Sometimes it takes me a while to figure things out. I can't even die right, for heaven's sake. Call me a slow learner, but you were no accident. When we got married, I didn't think Martin wanted to start a family, but he was totally fine with it."

"But what about your job, Ma?"

"My job was a job. I liked it. I was good at it. But, you know, I scarcely saw any of my co-workers after I retired. What does that tell you? It took me a while, but I finally figured out that what was most important to me was you and Martin. And if I hadn't waited so long and got so old, you'd have had siblings and they would have been important too. It's the love between us that's important." She looked at him a long moment. "I love you, Samuel. And I know you love Dee, so I love her to. I'm glad you have some of her family around. And I can't wait to see this baby."

A feeling of relief washed over Sam. He suddenly felt free, like a heavy weight he was carrying around had dissolved into nothing. He glanced at his mother with tears in his eyes, and reached for her hand grabbing only air.

"Hey where are you going? You just passed the main entrance for the hospital!"

Sam tapped the brakes, but then drove on. "They told us to use the second entrance. It's closer to maternity. I have no clue where I'm supposed to park though." He pulled into the first space that didn't say 'staff only' and sprinted toward the entrance. "Follow me if you want, but please, try to stay invisible!"

Birdie remained a misty shadow close behind him as Sam ran the gauntlet of admissions people. Another gatekeeper helped him garb up in paper over-shoes, a disposable cover-all gown and a floppy hat over his hair. Finally he was ushered into the room where Dee was.

"You made it! I'm so glad to see you!" Dee reached eagerly for his hand. "This really hurts, and they won't give me anything!"

Sam looked at Trish.

"Listen to Miss Impatient," Trish said sitting calmly beside her. "They just briefed her about her pain-control options. You barely made it in time, Sam. They'll be rolling her into delivery any minute."

It all happened fast after that. Sam took in everything, completely absorbed, wide-eyed and hyper-aware. He had no time to spare a thought for Birdie, a formless vapor hovering unseen near the ceiling.

Several hours later Dee lay tired but contented with the baby in her arms. "Everyone has been so great here. Especially that lactation consultant. I guess the fact that baby was hungry made everything easier." She smiled sleepily at Sam, whose tender gaze lingered on the delicate features of his newborn. He gently caressed the baby's cheek with his finger.

"How long are we going to call our child 'baby'?" he asked. "We agreed you get to name her. Have you thought of anything?"

"Of course I've thought of something! For the last however-many months I've been thinking about it. I want to name her Bridget."

Sam smiled. "I think she looks like a Bridget." He took her from Dee and cradled her in his arms.

Dee looked at them with eyes full of love. "And for short we can call her Birdie, after your mom."

Sam heard a soft gasp from near the ceiling. He closed his eyes and smiled, repeating the name 'Birdie.' Then he reached for Dee's hand. "I like that. I think my mother would like that too."

"You know what else?" Dee asked.

"What, Sweetheart." Sam couldn't imagine what might come next.

"I think we should get married at Chapel of the Winds."

Chapter 32

Birdie felt thrilled and elated and exhausted in a way she hadn't in a long time. And now that *little* Birdie was born she desperately wanted to see Martin to tell him the good news. She squeezed her eyes shut and said earnestly, "I want to go back to Fairlawn Street."

This time the motion felt more like an arcing swoop, like skimming down a sliding board. When it stopped Birdie found herself in the house on Fairlawn, on the couch in her living room. The moon shone dimly through the window blinds.

She drifted through the house and into the garage where Sam had moved her husband's recliner. "Martin," she called softly into the darkness.

"I'm right here Birdie."

"That's good," she said. "I have news for you. We have a granddaughter. Her name is Bridget."

"No kidding! A granddaughter." Birdie could hear the smile in his voice.

"And they're going to call her Birdie."

Martin chuckled. Birdie sat on the arm of the chair and took his hand in hers. "Martin, there's something else. I think it's time we left."

"You're probably right, Birdie."

She squeezed her eyes shut and concentrated on the place with the beautiful golden stars. "I want to go home," she said, and the two rose through the ceiling and disappeared.

* * *

Dee murmured reassuringly to the baby, fumbling with the release on the infant car seat while Sam unlocked the back door to the house and carried her things inside. He paused in the hallway to listen.

He hadn't thought about his mother since the evening before, when Dee told him the baby's name. Now he wondered. He took a few more steps, and listened again.

The house on Fairlawn Street was utterly silent.

His parents were gone.

The knowledge brought with it a sense of emptiness and loss.

Then, behind him, he heard a soft cry. The baby whimpered, and Dee cooed gently, "Hush, Birdie. Mommy's here. And look, here's your sweet little nursery."

Love and gratitude flooded Sam's soul. The house on Fairlawn Street did not feel empty anymore, and Sam was home.

THE END

ABOUT THE AUTHOR

Margaret Rodeheaver writes short fiction and novels for middle-grade and adult readers. She lives with her husband near Macon, Georgia, where she hangs out with various writers groups. She holds a bachelor's degree in journalism from the Ohio State University, and enjoys books, music, travel, and coffee. She is also a pretty good whistler. Visit www.Margaret-Rodeheaver.com to sign up for email updates about Margaret's latest books and the occasional freebie. You can also find her on Facebook and Instagram.

Also By Margaret Rodeheaver

Hidden Treasure (Chinkapin Series Book 1)

Finders Keepers (Chinkapin Series Book 2)

Second Home (Chinkapin Series Book 3)

Books For Kids By M. M. Rodeheaver

Haunted Holiday: a Christmas Cookie Ghost Story

The Ghost at Goblin's Glen

Porkington Hamm

Porkington Returns

Bonny's Debut

Porkington Hamm and the Lost Gold

Christmas Hamm: How Porkington Found the Holiday Spirit

Porkington Hamm and the Killer Tomatoes